The Stolen Bride

Hope's Crossing, Book 3

CYNTHIA WOOLF

Photo credits – Fotolia.com- pellinni; Adobe Stock - blackday

ISBN:
ISBN- 978-1-938887-76-5

DEDICATION

For Jim. Thanks for putting me to bed all those nights I fell asleep at my desk. Thank you for being my greatest cheerleader, my husband, my lover and my best friend.

I love you, sweetheart!

ACKNOWLEDGMENTS

For my Just Write partners Michele Callahan, Karen Docter, and Cate Rowan

For my wonderful cover artist, Romcon Custom Covers

For my wonderful editor, Linda Carroll-Bradd, you make my stories so much better.

CHAPTER 1

January 31, 1874
Hastings Ranch, Hope's Crossing, Montana Territory

"Alex, you've got to do something about those hellions of yours. Those girls need a mother."

"Now, Martha, they aren't that bad."

Alex stirred a teaspoon of sugar into his coffee. The sweet treat was one he looked forward to every morning.

Martha Jennings put the iron back on the stove and hung up the shirt she'd just pressed.

"They are. Those girls are four years old now and need to learn some manners. I know you feel like they got the raw end of the deal when Kate died, and you've done well alone up to this point, but if you don't do something soon, they will grow up thinking they can do anything they want. The first time someone says 'no' to them, that person will get shot with those slingshots they play with."

"A good thing they are independent little souls," countered Alex. "They have to be able to protect themselves. I won't always be here to do it for them."

"At this point it's the rest of us who need to be protected from those two uncouth little hooligans. Running through the house, chasing the dog, who they decided to give a bath. And, of course, since the dog is wet, they have to take all their clothes off and play in the tub with him!"

He shrugged and glanced outside at the snow on the ground, glistening in the sunshine. "They were outside and it was summer."

"Until he got loose when they tried to rinse him and ran through the house carrying pans of water. My nice clean house, I might add."

Alex chuckled. The complaint was old but the vision was still fresh in his memory. "They were cute as buttons running around bare-assed naked and you know it. Heck they were only three."

Martha shook her head but she smiled at the memory. "By the time I caught them and got the dog back outside, I was nearly as wet as they were."

"That you were."

"Listen to me, Alex Hastings." Martha wagged a finger at him. "You have to take them in hand or get someone in here who will. I can't be here all the time to do it. I have my own family to look after."

Alex sighed and ran a hand behind his neck. The realization that he needed to marry and get a mother for his girls made his chest ache. "I know Martha. I appreciate all the work you do. I can't expect you to raise my daughters as well. I guess it is time I remarried."

"Now you're talking sense. Why don't you get yourself one of those mail-order brides like Sam and Jesse did? You can't deny that Jo and Clare are wonderful women and you've never seen Sam or Jesse happier."

He nodded. What she said was true. He realized Sam and Jesse had never been happier. They both found love with their wives. Alex wouldn't. He wouldn't love again. It was too hard.

She reached into her apron pocket and pulled out a newspaper clipping.

"Here." She shoved the little piece of paper across the table to him. "I got this from Clare. It's for the agency both Sam and Jesse used."

Alex picked up the scrap of paper with a name and address and little else. *Matchmaker & Co, 467 10th Street, Golden, Colorado Territory. Contact Mrs. Maggie Black.*

"All right. I'll write to her and see what can be done. I don't want another wife, but I don't see a way around it. And finding one is impossible in Hope's Crossing where every female is either married, a prostitute, too old or too young."

Martha clasped Alex on the shoulder. "I know you miss Kate, but this is the right thing to do for those girls. You'll see."

"I hope you're right. You know I'd do anything for Rose and Violet."

"I know." She moved back to the ironing board and started on the next piece of clothing. "The hardest thing will be to stand with their new mother when she disciplines them. That'll be hard for you to do because you don't want to see them unhappy, but it's necessary. They'll thank you for it…eventually."

Alex nodded and left the kitchen. He had let the girls run roughshod over everyone including him. Their mama dying was his fault. He never should have kept that stallion. He'd been too much animal for Kate to handle but she'd begged and promised she wouldn't let him have his head. Alex had still said no, but she took the animal out anyway before Alex could stop her. The horse knew its rider was inexperienced and took off…a runaway.

Then the stupid animal had stopped dead at the fallen tree in his way instead of jumping over it. Kate had flown over his head and broken her neck.

That was two years ago. Now his girls were acting like that animal, wild and untamed. He didn't want to have to cage them, like he had the stallion. No one rode the big black. No one could handle him except Alex, who was afraid he'd take out his temper on the animal and so left him alone in his stall or the corral.

The only time he was with other horses

was during breeding. Alex had gotten a couple of very good colts and several fillies off of the black horse.

Kate had called him Beauty.

Alex called him the Beast.

*****

The music was lovely, the food scrumptious, and mostly, the company was engaging, but Isabella Latham was bored. Every week was the same, visiting the New York City hospitals, taking luncheon with her mother's friends, followed by the only thing she enjoyed. Riding hell bent for leather on her hunter, Champion. He was temperamental and barely broken to the saddle, but she loved riding him. Every Saturday she took him out for two or three hours, as long as she could get away with. The outings were the only time she felt free.

Tonight was another of Ernst and Julia Latham's balls. Isabella had a new dress made for it. The beautiful pale pink gown of the finest silk had three rows of ruffles on the under skirt and looked wonderful with her pale skin, brandy-brown eyes and hair. The over shirt was smooth and gathered in the back over the bustle, the gathering held with ribbons of satin anchored in a choker around her neck. She had to admit the design of the dress was what drew her because the satin ribbons attached to the collar made it look like she was being strangled, when she was not. The shock she saw on people faces when they saw her in the dress was worth the cost.

The bodice was perfectly fitted over her tightest corset and showed only a bit of décolletage from the off-shoulder design.

Beautiful as it was, she hadn't looked forward to wearing it. Isabella couldn't breathe in the dang thing and she swore the lack of air kept her brain from functioning correctly. Otherwise she wouldn't have just heard her father say he was announcing her engagement. To whom?

"Ladies and gentlemen, friends and colleagues, I would like to take this opportunity to announce the engagement of my daughter, Isabella, to my business associate, Mr. Sydney Rockwell."

Her father was rather red in the face. Perhaps he'd overindulged, and that was the reason for such an announcement. Surely, her mother would take him in hand and correct this outrageous situation. But, when she looked at her mother she saw fire in her mother's emerald eyes and a rather pained smile on Julia's normally lovely face.

Suddenly, Sydney Rockwell, a large, fat man, who was at least three inches shorter than Bella, was at her side.

"Come, my dear, smile. It's your engagement party after all."

He took her, none too gently, by the elbow and guided her to where her parents stood on the bandstand.

"Smile," he whispered and squeezed her elbow painfully.

She obeyed.

He eased his grip but didn't let her go completely.

"We are very happy," said Sydney to the crowd of suddenly interested people. "And we will be married in two weeks' time at St. Patrick's Cathedral. Of course, you are all invited and I hope you will attend."

He smiled.

"Smile, my dear," he said out of the side of his mouth while he kept what looked to her like a maniacal grin on his face.

He again squeezed her arm.

She smiled, grimaced was more like it, but the gesture soothed him and he released her.

Hours later, the party was finally over and all the guests were gone.

"Come to the library, Isabella." Her father made the statement with some resignation.

She followed him and found her mother there waiting.

"I know this was somewhat of a surprise," her father began as he seated himself in the large leather chair behind the massive mahogany desk. "But you must see this through. You see, I owe Rockwell a lot of money. Money I don't have and won't have any time soon."

"So you what? Sold me to him instead?"

"He wanted you and said he would cancel the debt if you became his wife. So you will marry him."

"Regardless of the fact he's old enough to be my father and I find the man totally repugnant?!" Isabella paced in front of her father's desk. He hadn't imbibed too much. This was what he had planned for her future—marriage to the most hideous man on the planet.

"Yes, and stop shouting." Her father shouted back. Then he said in a calmer voice, "You will maintain a dignified tone when speaking to me, or you will not speak."

Isabella closed her eyes and took as deep and calming a breath as her corset would allow her. "So, my feelings in this matter mean nothing?"

He steepled his hands on top of the desk. "No. They do not. You will do as you are told."

"May I leave now?"

"Yes." Her father waved her away. "Go to your room."

Her mother had said nothing during the exchange. Isabella looked over at her. But her mother didn't look back. How could she let him do this? She knew her parents weren't close. In fact, she was surprised they remained married but this, this complete betrayal by her mother surprised her.

"And you, Mother? You go along with this…atrocity?"

Her mother did not look at Isabella. "Yes. Go to your room. I'll come help you remove your dress shortly."

"Don't bother. Lucy will help me."

"I gave Lucy the night off. She's visiting her sister in New York."

Isabella nodded curtly and left the room.

She managed to keep her back stick-straight until she closed the door to the library behind her. Then she sagged against it. How could her parents do this to her? Sell her, and to Sydney Rockwell, of all people.

She lifted her skirts and ran from the library all the way up the stairs to her room, where she threw herself face first on the bed and cried. Isabella had never felt so betrayed in her life.

A while later, she didn't know how much time had passed, she heard the door open and then close with a click.

"Bella, my sweet darling. I'm sorry Ernst has done this. I couldn't stop what happened tonight, but listen to me for I might have found a way out of this marriage. I won't let you marry that evil man. It's said he bought his wife at fourteen from her father and she committed suicide to escape him. Personally, I believe he murdered her. Either way, he's a depraved man."

Isabella, Bella to those who loved her, raised her head, her eyes gritty from crying and then sat up on the side of the bed.

"How? How can I get out of this?"

"Here, read this."

Her mother handed over a clipping from the newspaper out of the envelope she carried, and sat next to her.

Bella looked at the piece of paper—an ad for mail-order brides.

Wanted. Upstanding women for marriage to like-minded men in the West. Ranchers, miners and other professional men in the Montana Territory await you. Apply to Matchmaker & Co., Mrs. Maggie Black at the Golden, Colorado office or Miss Susan Wyatt at the New York office.

She let the paper drop and turned toward her mother. "How will this help me?"

"I thought to put you on a train to Denver, Colorado and have you check out the prospective grooms from the Golden office. That will get you out of town immediately. You won't be able to take along much. Two valises at the most, so pack your plainest, most serviceable dresses and undergarments. Wear your riding boots because slippers are worthless when you have to be outside for extended periods of time."

"Why are you doing this? I thought you were in agreement with Father."

Her mother jumped up and began pacing

from the bed to the door and back again. "Never! Sydney Rockwell is a vile, hideous man, who took advantage of Ernst's weakness for gambling and got us in this mess. He's always wanted you and finally found a way to accomplish that. But I won't let this marriage happen."

As she listened, a kernel of hope bloomed in Bella's chest. She had never seen her mother this upset.

"Won't I just be going from one unwanted marriage to another with this mail-order bride solution?"

"That's why I'm sending you to Golden. You may at least be able to pick a man who doesn't repulse you. Being in the West means time will pass before Ernst can find you. But he, or more likely Sidney Rockwell, will find you. You must be married, and the marriage consummated, before you're safe. I overheard the conversation between Ernst and Sydney. He wants your virginity, you see. He's a truly evil and despicable man."

She'd never been farther from home than Aunt Agatha's in Brooklyn. And the West? She'd heard horrific stories about the West and how dangerous it was. Still she'd rather face that than marry Sydney Rockwell. "How am I leaving without Father knowing and sending someone to stop me?"

"I'm telling Ernst you have the chicken pox. He's never had them, so he won't want to see you for at least two weeks. I'm telling him you are contagious and I'm having Lucy stay at her sister's home. I'm sorry my darling, that's all the headstart I can give you. But I hope it is enough so you can disappear into the wilds of Montana and out of Ernst's or Sydney's grasp."

Isabella wrung her hands together. "Does that mean I'll never see you again?"

Julia moved to the bed and sat next to Isabella. "More than likely. But you know I will always be with you."

Her mother touched Isabella's chest over her heart.

"In here."

Isabella burst into tears, her hands over her face.

Her mother sat beside her and held her.

Isabella felt closer to her mother than she had since she was a child.

"Hush, now my love. You'll be fine. You're a strong woman, my darling daughter. No one thought you would be able to ride that hunter of yours—that he was too wild, but you did and you still do. Use those strengths and you'll be just fine."

Bella sat up and wiped her cheeks with the palms of her hands.

"Thank you, Mama. I will be the best wife to whomever I choose that they can possibly want." *I can arrange flowers and fold the napkins for dinner. I'll learn whatever else I need to learn.* "I'll make you proud of me."

"I'm already proud. Now pack your things. You leave at first light."

Julia reached into the envelope and removed several pieces of paper.

"Here are your tickets to Golden, Colorado. You'll have to find Matchmaker & Co. when you get there and make your match as quickly as possible. I've already written to Mrs. Maggie Black, in your name, of course. She knows you will be arriving by train on February 16th. I've asked her to arrange a room for you, and she agreed. All you will have to do is make your match. In here," she held out the envelope to Bella. "I have put everything you'll need and all the money I had stashed away from your father—one thousand dollars. That should last you for a good long while, if need be. Also included are the letters from Mrs. Black answering my questions, so you can get familiar with what she wrote."

"Thank you, Mama." Isabella forced a smile knowing her mother was as sad as she was at her upcoming departure. "Thank you so much. And I will see you again. After I'm married and settled, I'll bring your first grandchild to see you."

Smiling, Julia wrapped her arms around Bella.

"I will love that and can't wait for that day. Now, get packed. Remember, only serviceable clothes. Plain dresses and include your riding outfit. You may find it useful."

Her mind was in a whirl. "How will I get to the train station?"

Julia loosened her embrace on Bella. "I've arranged with Peter Farnsworth to come and get you. He'll be here in just two hours."

"Farnsworth? But he hates Father, why would he help you?"

"Because he hates Ernst, not me, and helping you is something that would get back at Ernst. He'll never tell where he's taken you." She cupped her hands on Bella's shoulders. "Believe me when I say he wants only what is best for you."

She frowned and searched her mother's expression for clues. "That's very odd, but I believe you. He's always been kind to me. Nicer than Father ever was."

"I know." Julia looked away toward the window.

Something wasn't right. Her mother was hiding a truth, but Bella didn't have time to think about what that could be. The time was already past two in the morning and she had to pack very judiciously if she was to get the most out of her two bags.

An hour and a half later, she was ready. Wearing her blue wool traveling suit, black wool coat and riding boots, she could handle anything that might arise.

Julia helped her down the back stairs and out of the door.

As arranged, a Farnsworth surrey, recognizable by the eagle on the side, awaited her. Peter Farnsworth himself was driving the sleek carriage. After a nod, he came forward, took the bags from Bella and put them in the backseat. Then he waited to help her onto the front seat beside him.

Bella turned to her mother and gave her a hug. "Remember what I said. I'll be back."

"Yes, my darling daughter. I'll be waiting."

Peter walked to her mother. "It's not too late, Julia. You could go, too."

"No. Bella has a better chance to get away from Ernst without me."

He took her mother's hand, kissed the top, and then turned it over to kiss the underside of her wrist.

Eyes wide, Bella wondered, not for the first time, if Peter Farnsworth didn't love her mother. He was a very attractive man, tall with brown hair and eyes, but had never married. Whenever her mother gazed at Peter, she had a certain look about her...one of longing. A story definitely existed between them, but for now, Bella would just have to wonder what it was.

Her mother stood on the porch and watched at least until the carriage was out of sight. Bella knew, because she had viewed her mother until she could see her no more.

"Are you ready, Miss Latham?" asked Mr. Farnsworth.

"Ready?"

"For your life to begin."

"Oh, yes. I'm more than ready."

Bella turned and faced forward, watching the buildings go by. She didn't look back. Her life was ahead of her, perhaps for the first time, and she embraced the possibilities.

CHAPTER 2

February 16, 1874

Bella stood on the street looking at the robin's egg blue door behind which was the office of Matchmaker & Co. She'd actually found the place and tears threatened to fall but she blinked them back. She ran a hand over her hair and patted the bun at her nape, then took a deep breath and turned the knob.

The inside was bright. The large picture window, though covered with a sheer curtain, provided plenty of light. In the front of the room was an oval braided rug, with a sofa and two wing chairs on it. The back of the sofa faced the door. Bella set her valises near the wall to the side of the door.

Toward the rear of the room was a single

light wood desk, a pretty woman with dark red hair sat in the large leather chair behind it. Two tables with boxes on top were next to the wall behind the chair.

"Mrs. Black?" Bella asked of the woman.

"Yes, I'm Maggie Black. How can I help you?"

"I'm Isabella Latham. I believe you were expecting me."

"Oh, yes, Isabella. Sit there." She pointed at the sofa. "Let's be comfortable."

Bella sat with her hands around her reticule resting in her lap.

Maggie came forward and sat next to her. "Tell me why you're so anxious for a marriage? I know what '*you*' wrote but I want to hear it in your own words. I don't believe your letters were actually from you but *from* someone who loves you."

The dam broke. The thought of her mother, so far away in New York, and the sacrifices she'd made for Bella made her tears flow. She told Mrs. Black everything.

Maggie frowned. "I see. Do you believe you would be putting anyone else in danger?"

"No. Their only reason for coming is to

find me."

"Good. I've got several prospects: a farmer in Kansas, a miner in Montana and a rancher also in Montana. I believe the rancher is your correct match. He is looking for a wife and mother for his two little girls. They are four years old and need someone who can bring them under control."

Bella shook her head. "Why would you think he would be a good match for me? I don't have children. Don't have any idea how to raise them."

"Yes, you do. You know how you were raised. They need someone to take them in hand and show them how to be ladies."

"They are only four." Bella remembered when she was that age. Her mother had given Bella her first pony, Socks. She'd named him because he was black except for four white legs. She'd had to learn the capitals of all thirty-seven states before she could sit on the pony's back.

"Yes, but it's never too soon to learn. I've discovered that in the raising of my own children."

"How many children do you have?"

"I have two so far. A girl and a boy. They are nine and two."

"What if the girls hate me?"

"Oh, they are liable to in the beginning, but I know you can get over that. My oldest, is actually my step-daughter. Though I suppose she never hated me. Just the opposite in fact. She was thrilled to have another woman in the house. Her words not mine."

Maggie smiled.

"Is the rancher far away?"

"The farthest. He's got a large ranch near Hope's Crossing in the very western part of the Montana Territory. Getting there is actually quite a trip."

Good. The farther away the better. "Then he's the one I choose."

"Very good. I believe this is a good match for you and you'll be happy. Let me get his file and you can see what he looks like. He's very handsome in my opinion. Reminds me of my own husband."

The door opened and a tall, dark-haired man came in.

"Ah, I was just speaking of you."

Maggie walked over to the man. He put his arms around her waist, bent down and kissed her.

"I hope you were saying nice things."

"Oh, she was," said Bella. They appeared to be very happy. Bella hoped she could find that kind of happiness for herself…in Montana Territory.

"Caleb, this is Isabella Latham, my latest client."

The man walked over to the sofa and put out his hand.

Bella took it and he gave her a firm handshake.

"Caleb Black, Maggie's husband. Pleased to meet you."

He returned to his wife's side.

"What are you doing in town?" asked Maggie, gazing up at her husband.

"I had some business at the bank and wanted to see if you would like to have lunch with me."

"Not today, dear. I have business to attend to."

"Very well. I'll head back to the ranch then. Nice to meet you, Miss Latham."

He tipped his hat, gave his wife another kiss and took his leave.

Maggie returned to the couch with the file.

"I hope you didn't mind the disruption."

"Not at all. Your husband seems a very

nice man and handsome, too."

"He is. Speaking of which, here is the picture of Mr. Alexander Hastings." Maggie extended her hand with the photograph to Bella. "He has two daughters, Rose and Violet."

The photograph was of a man sitting in a chair with a little girl standing on either side. He was wearing a three-piece suit and well-tied cravat. Each of the girls had on a dress with three layers of ruffles in the skirt.

Maggie hadn't been exaggerating. He was very handsome, with dark hair and mustache. His hair was just a little too long and, though combed behind his ears, she still saw the curls at the ends.

The girls had dark hair like their father, hanging in braids on either side of their heads. And probably brown eyes, though she was guessing.

Still she was filled with doubt. What if she got there and he didn't want to marry her?

"Mrs. Black—"

"Call me, Maggie."

"Maggie, what if I get there and Mr. Hastings changes his mind? What am I to do then?"

Maggie leaned over and put her hand on Bella's knee.

"First, that won't happen. But if it did, Mr. Hastings has to pay for your stay at the hotel until you can take the return stage. He sent enough money to cover your stay here in Golden at the Astor House, the train to Cheyenne and the stage to Hope's Crossing. So you have nothing to worry about. Trust me. I'm very certain of this match and I've not been wrong yet."

"He has kind eyes. His daughters look adorable and well cared for. I'm willing if he's willing to marry me."

"Good. I was fairly sure, after reading your mother's letters and knowing she was not who she claimed, that you would be the one showing up today. A mother will go to any lengths to save her child. But based on the information she gave me, which was quite accurate by the way, I took the liberty of writing to Mr. Hastings and accepted his proposal on your behalf."

"Is that unusual?"

"Oh, yes." Maggie gave a curt nod. "I've only done it on very rare occasions. After hearing the full story from you, I think it's good I did."

"When will I be leaving for Montana?"

"On tomorrow's train. You'll need only one night at the Astor House but I know you'll be comfortable there. The train ride will not be too bad, but I'm afraid the stagecoach, which takes seven or eight days will not be much fun."

"I'll manage. I'm really not a delicate person, though my mother may have led you to believe otherwise."

"No, actually, I got the impression you are quite self-sufficient and learn quickly, which is probably a good thing. I would imagine you'll have many things to learn in order to live on a ranch. It will be quite different than living in New York society believe me."

"You came from New York, too?"

"I did. Before my first husband died, we were regular members of the societal rounds of balls and dinner parties. There won't be any of that there."

"What about horseback riding? Will I be able to do that out here?"

"I would think so, but that is something you will have to discuss with your husband. Now, let's get these papers signed and get you settled for the night. You'll have to be up early in the morning to catch the train to Denver and then the one to Cheyenne."

She looked down at the watch pinned to her dress.

"You'll have to be up at four o'clock in the morning. The first train to Denver leaves at five."

Isabella nodded as she walked to the desk. "I will be there. Thank you, Maggie. You're saving my life."

Maggie accepted the signed contract. "Always glad to help a young woman in need. Come now. I'll walk you to the Astor House."

Isabella held the envelope with all the information from Maggie close to her chest. She'd read over each document when she got to her room.

"Is the Astor House a boarding house, or do I need to find some place to eat?"

"It is a boarding house and we should be getting you there in time for lunch."

"Wonderful. I'm starving."

*****

March 1, 1874

The train to Cheyenne had been quite nice. The seats were padded and she'd been lucky enough to have the entire bench to herself so she could spread out.

Then came the stage ride which was a complete nightmare. Six passengers from Cheyenne to Bozeman. No one could move. Or breathe. The cramped quarters did keep everyone warmer, though and for that she was grateful.

The countryside they drove through was covered in snow and flat, though she could see mountains in the distance to the West. Everyone was thrilled to come to a stage stop and always hopeful someone would be getting off for good but no one did. One cowboy rode up top with his saddle because there was no room inside the coach.

When the rest of the people got off at Bozeman, the blond cowboy sat inside with Bella.

"Howdy, miss. I'm Jackson Bryant, but folks just call me Jack B. There's usually another Jack, it's a common name."

Bella held out her gloved hand. "Bella Latham. I'm going to Hope's Crossing. Where are you headed?"

"Hope's Crossing and the Hastings ranch. Got me a job busting 'tangs."

"I'm hopefully heading to the Hastings

ranch myself. I'm to marry Mr. Hastings when I reach Hope's Crossing. What do you do? Busting what?"

His blue eyes sparkled with pride. "Bronc busting mustangs. Breaking them to the saddle so they can be ridden."

"Oh, I see. I love to ride."

Jack B smiled. "You one of them mail-order brides?"

Bella bowed her head, her cheeks heating. "Yes. I'm a mail-order bride."

"Those men back home must have been blind to let you get away."

She raised her head. "Thank you Mr. Bryant. That's very kind of you to say."

"I call 'em like I see 'em. You're way too pretty to be a mail-order bride."

She hoped Alexander Hastings felt the same way. "I'm rather plain compared to the ladies back home. That's why I never married. Plus the one person who did want to marry me, I found totally repulsive. He was nearly thirty years older than me."

Jack B stuck his head out the window and spit.

"Forgive me, Miss Bella. That was uncouth of me."

"That's all right. I've wanted to do the

same to get the dust out of my mouth, but found I didn't have any spit to spit."

Jack B held up a metal container with a lid attached with a chain closing the top.

"It's not cold but it's wet. Get that dust right out of there."

Bella took the offering and put it to her lips. The water was heavenly. She was so thirsty but she only took a couple of swallows.

"Thank you so much. I think the company should require everyone on a stage ride should have one of those." She pointed at the silver container.

"It's called a canteen."

"Yes, everyone should have to have a canteen before boarding the stage. We'd all be more comfortable and perhaps less cranky if we weren't so thirsty." The coach ride was less smooth since they'd left Bozeman. The roads were obviously rougher. She wished the seats had been padded, but her backside was more numb than anything now, so at this late date it wouldn't have mattered. The scenery was beautiful. They were headed farther into the mountains and patches of snow covered the hillsides. Small groves of trees dotted the landscape. She imagined it would be quite lovely, covered in with green grass and flowers like the scenes in the paintings at the Astor House

"You could be right about that, Miss Bella. Mind if I stretch my legs onto the other half of your seat?"

"No, not at all."

She moved her skirt to make more room for him.

"I'm too tall for riding in a stage. That's why I don't mind riding up top with the gear. I can spread these long ol' legs of mine."

"Yes, you do appear to be quite tall."

"I'm six feet six inches and mostly leg. That's why I'm good at busting broncs. I can hang on better because my legs are so long."

"Yes, I can see you being good at that."

Someone pounded on the roof.

"Hope's Crossing coming up," shouted the driver.

Bella stuck her face out the window in an effort to see the town. She knew it was supposed to be small; nothing like New York City, but what she saw dismayed her. The town she saw was not even as big as

Golden had been.

There were several mostly one-story buildings lining the street. The largest building was only three stories. The coach slowed as it approached that building and then stopped right in front.

Jack B opened the door and hopped down. Then he held out his hand to help Bella down.

"Thank you, Jack B."

The shotgun rider tossed down her bags and Jack B caught them for her.

"Here you go, Miss Bella."

He put her valises next to her on the boardwalk.

Jack B's saddle and saddle bags were handed down to him, not tossed. Now that she could see the saddle, she realized it was a work of art in leather. The leather had been carved and worked into intricate designs which she didn't recognize. And she could tell by the sheen where Jack B brushed off the dust that the saddle was well cared for.

"That's a beautiful saddle."

"Thank you, Miss. I try to keep it in good shape. It's my tool for making a living. Without it, I'm not nearly as effective. This saddle was made specifically for me by a man outside Taos, New Mexico. I've had it for nearly ten years now."

Bella stepped away from the coach, farther onto the boardwalk and began to look around.

"Have you met Mr. Hastings before, Jack B?"

He nodded. "Sure have. Worked for him last year. He'll be here shortly. His ranch is outside of Hope's Crossing about ten miles."

"Oh, I thought it was closer than that."

"Nope. But everyone comes to town on Saturday, so you won't be totally isolated at the ranch."

The sign on the building said Hope's Crossing Hotel and it seemed to be the hub of the city, though she couldn't really call Hope's Crossing a city. Bella looked around at everyone coming and going on the sidewalk, their boots and shoes striking the surface and sounding like an army, though there were only eight or ten people who milled about in front of the hotel. Most were getting ready to board the stage. The driver collected tickets. The ladies she saw wore simple wool coats and bonnets. No one wore a hat like the feathered one she wore.

"Here he comes now."

CHAPTER 3

Jack B pointed down the walkway to a tall, man dressed in black coat, black pants, black hat and gloves.

Bella put a hand on her stomach in an attempt to quell the butterflies fluttering there. The feeling had started as soon as she'd seen the town from the top of the hill and had been building during the ride. She'd tried to ignore it, to no avail. She was glad she was wearing gloves so he wouldn't know her palms were moist.

"Don't be scared Miss Bella. Alex Hastings is a good man."

"Thank you, Jack B. I'll try to remember that."

The man in question stopped in front of

them and extended a hand to the cowboy.

"Hello, Jack B. Glad to see you. We've got a fine lot of horses that need your expertise."

"Good," Jack B smiled. "You know how I like to work."

The man nodded and then he turned to her.

"Isabella Latham?"

She looked up into his deep, clear blue gaze.

"Y…yes. I'm Isabella."

Giving a smile, he held out his hand to her.

"I'm Alex Hastings. Pleased to meet you, Miss Latham."

She put her hand in his and it was swallowed by his big one.

"The pleasure is mine, Mr. Hastings."

"Did you have a good trip here?"

"As well as can be expected I would imagine. It's no small feat to get to Hope's Crossing."

He laughed.

The deep, rich sound pleased her.

"Are you ready to get married?"

"Now? This minute? I thought we'd have some time before we go to the church."

"We're getting married by the judge, not the reverend. Does that make a difference to you?"

"No, not really." She paused and swallowed hard. "I'm a bit nervous."

"Understandable. We must return to the ranch today, so we have to marry before that. Are you ready?"

Bella took a deep breath. "Yes, I am."

"Good. Let's go. Jack B can be one of our witnesses. Right, Jack B?"

Jack B swung his saddle over his shoulder. "Sure thing, boss."

Alex eyed the valises at her feet. "Are these bags yours? Should I be looking for a trunk?"

Isabella shook her head. "Just these two."

Alex picked them both up with one hand and put his arm out toward her.

"We'll go see the judge now, get married, and then we'll head home to the ranch. My girls are excited to meet you."

She rested her hand in the crook of his arm as they walked down the boardwalk. "They are? I'm anxious to meet them, but I thought there would mostly be resentment on their part to have someone who might come between them and you."

"Let's get this straight at the start." Alex stopped walking and faced her. "My girls are running wild. I know this and I will stand with you when you need to rein them in some. I've been lax in their discipline and will probably continue to be, but as long as you are fair and take their welfare to heart, you will have my support."

"Thank you. The best I can do is raise them the way my mother raised me. After I've been here for a while, I expect them to be polite and ladylike most of the time. I realize they are still just little girls but, for instance, when we have company I expect them to be on their best behavior."

He raised an eyebrow. "We don't have company very often so I expect them to be better behaved more often than that."

They walked from the hotel two blocks east and then crossed the street to the courthouse. Entering the courthouse Alex walked directly to the office of Nathaniel Harden, Justice of the Peace.

He opened the door, entered and said, "Good afternoon, Clarence. Is the judge in?"

The skinny young man with blond hair and glasses looked up from the papers he was writing on.

"Good afternoon, Mr. Hastings. He's in and has been expecting you. I've got the marriage license ready to go. I just need to put in your full names." He pulled a sheet from the wooden tray on his desk.

"Alexander Franklin Hastings," said Alex as he watched Clarence write on the paper.

Clarence dipped his pen in the inkwell on his desk and looked up at Bella, eyebrows raised.

"Isabella Louise Latham," she said quickly.

"Thank you both. If you'll follow me."

Clarence went through the door behind his desk. In the office a rotund man with gray hair and beard sat behind the desk. He looked up when they entered.

"Good to see you, Alex."

The judge held out his hand.

Alex shook it.

"You too, Nate. I don't see you often enough when I come to town. Just at the monthly poker game. Unless we happen to run into each other at the mercantile. I guess, in a way, that's good." He chuckled. "It means I've been keeping out of trouble."

The judge laughed. "That's true." His attention turned to Bella. "Who do we have here?"

"Isabella Latham, your honor."

He took Bella's hand in both of his.

"We don't stand on ceremony here, Miss Latham. I'm just Nate."

"Very nice to meet you, Nate. And so I'm Bella."

"Very good. Isabella is much too staid for this part of the country. We're pretty laid back here."

Alex looked over and grinned.

Bella stomach did a little flip.

"I like you Bella. Let's get you married to Alex, here, before I decide to marry you myself."

"Get your own bride," said Alex with half a smile.

Nate looked up at Jack B.

"Who are you my tall, lanky friend?"

"Jack Bryant, judge. I work for Mr. Hastings as a bronc buster."

"Well today you are a witness to their marriage."

"Yes, sir. Be my honor."

"Let's get started," said Alex. "I've got to get home to my daughters."

Nate smiled indulgently.

"How are those two little hoydens?"

"Driving everyone crazy as usual. But that's about to change. Bella will see to that."

Bella gave him a tentative smile and hoped he was right. Hoped his trust wasn't misplaced, and she could help these little girls grow into polite young ladies.

"All right, enough gab. Let's get down to business," said Nate. "Jack B, you and Clarence are the witnesses."

"Yes, sir, judge." Jack B took off his hat and set it on one of the chairs against the wall. "Ready when you are."

"Fine." Nate opened his bible and began to read. "We are gathered here in the presence of these witnesses to join this man and this woman in holy matrimony..."

Bella tried to concentrate on the words being spoken by Nate but found herself thinking about the ceremony. This definitely wasn't the wedding of her dreams. She'd always imagined she'd be wearing a flowing white dress and carrying a bouquet of yellow roses instead she found herself mesmerized by a pair of sky blue eyes locked with her brown ones.

Nate stopped and looked at her.

She looked back, lost.

"This is the part where you say, 'I do'," said Nate gently.

"I do," she uttered quickly.

He repeated the words for Alex who responded with a firm, 'I do'. His deep baritone voice made her insides quiver.

"By the power vested in me by the town of Hope's Crossing, the Territory of Montana and the United States government, I now pronounce you man and wife. You may kiss your bride." Nate beamed at them.

Alex bent down and placed his lips on hers.

Bella closed her eyes and pursed her lips.

Alex chuckled.

Her eyes flew open.

He placed his hands on either side of her head and his lips over hers. He pressed his tongue against her lips.

She gasped.

Alex took advantage and plunged into her mouth. He explored, dueled with her tongue and finally retreated.

She'd never been kissed like that before. Every other kiss she'd received paled in comparison to the one her husband had just given her. Would that be the way he always kissed her? She certainly hoped so.

"I hope you both have a wonderful life together," said Nate, a wide smile lighting up his face.

"Thanks, Nate."

Alex pressed a double eagle gold piece into the judge's hand.

"I don't charge that much, only five dollars, but I appreciate the extra," he said as his hand quickly closed over the coin.

Alex laughed and clapped the judge on the back.

"I'll get it back at the next poker game."

Judge Harden cocked an eyebrow.

"Don't be so sure. Your luck can't hold much longer."

"We'll see."

Alex put his hand at Bella's waist and guided her to the door.

"Nice to meet you, Judge Harden," she said before Alex whisked her out the door, into the outer office and then the hall.

"Are you hungry?" he asked. "The ride to the house will take about an hour and a half. Then we can eat or we can eat now."

"Will I be expected to cook when we get

to your house?"

"Depends on if Martha fixed supper or Cookie the trail cook did. If Cookie did, then yes, you'll have to cook."

"Then I'd rather eat here. I am hungry. Jack B and I haven't eaten since the last stage stop before dawn this morning."

"Well then let's get you two fed."

He led the way back to the Hope's Crossing Hotel and the restaurant there.

When they reached the bright yellow building with white trim, Alex ushered them inside to the eatery.

A little, tiny lady, no more than five feet tall, with snow white hair pulled up into a bun on top of her head, greeted them as they entered.

"Good morning, Alexander. Who have you got there with you?"

"Good morning, Effie. This is my wife, Bella and my bronc buster."

"Bella, this is Iphigenia Smith, but we all call her Effie."

"Is that tall drink of water, Jack B?" replied the little woman, looking way up at Jack B's smiling face.

"Yes, ma'am, Miss Effie. It's me."

"Bend down here and give me some

sugar."

Jack B obediently bent nearly in half and kissed the woman on the cheek.

"And you're Bella Hastings." She looked Bella up and down. "My Alexander's new wife. You're a mail-order bride aren't you? We have two others in our town, Jo Longworth and Clare Donovan. You'll have to meet them. Wonderful ladies. Now, would you all like a table by the window or one farther inside?"

"Inside, I think," said Alex.

"Yes, please. I'd rather not be on display." Bella said as she crushed her cloth reticule in her hands. She hastily added, "as I eat."

"I never thought of it that way," said Effie. "No wonder no one wants to sit at those tables."

"If you close the curtains, I'm sure they would be fine," said Bella.

"Good idea," agreed Effie.

She showed them to a square table with a red-and-white-checked table cloth, set for four, in the middle of the room. Effie removed the fourth place setting and set it on an adjacent table.

"Do you want your usual, Alex? Steak,

mashed potatoes, gravy, peas, and apple pie for dessert?" asked Effie, taking a small pad out of the pocket of her apron.

"Yes ma'am. That'll do me fine."

Effie turned to Bella. "What about you, dearie?"

"I'll take the same as Alex, please."

Bella's mouth watered. She was starving, hadn't had a decent meal since she left Golden, more than a week ago. The fare at the way stations was usually beans from a large pot with slices of bread. Not that it was bad…well, yes it was bad. But the food had filled the void in her stomach and for that she was grateful.

"How about you, cowboy?"

"Might as well make it three, Miss Effie."

Effie wrote on the little pad of paper.

"You folks are just too easy on me. I didn't have to recite the other selections and I appreciate it."

Effie chuckled and walked back toward the kitchen.

"I'm glad to see you have a healthy appetite," said Alex. "I don't believe you can do the work you'll be doing eating like a bird."

"Just what do you expect from me besides raising your children?" said Bella.

Effie returned with three cups in one hand, a coffee pot hanging off that arm and a plate with slices of bread and butter on it in the other hand. She set down the cups, then the bread and filled cups from the pot.

"There's cream on the table," she said before turning and walking back to the kitchen.

Jack B grabbed a slice of the bread and buttered it.

"Excuse my manners," said Jack B. "My stomach is so empty it thinks my throat's been cut."

"Don't worry," said Bella. "Eat what you want. They can always bring more."

Jack B took another slice and then passed the bread to Alex.

Alex took a piece and then set the bread plate on the table in front of Bella.

She watched him, unable to look away from his deep blue eyes. He in turn watched her, barely looking at the food he set on the table.

Effie returned with their meals, setting one large platter sized plate in front of each of them.

The spell was broken.

After gazing at the food, Bella looked up at Effie. "Thank you. This looks wonderful." She took a bite of the fluffy mashed potatoes and couldn't help the yummy sound that came out.

Alex chuckled.

She swallowed and then smiled. "Excuse me. I'm hungrier than I thought."

"I can tell by the way Jack B has nearly cleaned his plate already."

Alex jutted his chin toward Jack B.

"Sorry, boss. I'm still just a growin' boy," Jack B said with a rakish smile.

Jack B was a handsome man by anyone's standards. Golden blond hair and blue eyes were nice, but when he smiled, and those dimples showed...goodness.

As it was, her husband's smoldering dark, good looks were almost too much. Bella couldn't imagine how she'd gotten so lucky. When Alex smiled, his teeth white against his dark mustache, he was definitely worth her faint, had she been that kind of woman.

She just hoped her husband was as passionate as his kiss made her feel he was, for she had to seduce him tonight. They must consummate the marriage. She could not remain a virgin, just in case her father found her.

After they finished dining, Alex took them to the wagon. He'd brought the buckboard in anticipation of needing it to carry home Bella's trunk, or trunks. As it was, Jack B rode in back with the luggage and was able to stretch his legs for the long ride. He used his saddle as a pillow, pulled his hat down over his face and fell asleep.

It was cold out and she was happy she'd worn her heavy wool coat. Bella wouldn't have minded having something more comfortable to sit on than just the plank of wood. The seat was narrow. Her leg touched Alex's and her skirt fell over his right leg. She pulled it aside but it fell right back because of all her petticoats.

"Leave it," he said, placing his hand on top of hers. "It's just going to keep falling over anyway. The seat is almost too narrow for two people to sit on. Besides we'll both be covered with that blanket you're getting from under the seat."

"I am? Oh, yes, I am." Bella reached under the seat and found two blankets. She took one and handed it back to Jack B.

"Here you go. This should help you keep warm."

Jack B accepted the blanket and unfolded it to cover as much of him as possible.

She took the second blanket and laid it across both her and Alex's laps.

"We're lucky snows not falling. It would be a miserable ride."

"I suppose that's true. Tell me about your daughters. Other than being a bit on the wild side and out of control, what else should I know?"

"They are actually the sweetest girls. They love everybody and there's not a mean bone in either one of them, but they do like to play jokes on people. Pranks some would call them. Like putting a live frog in my bed. They get into trouble for little things, like making mud pies in the kitchen." He smiled.

"I can't imagine ever doing that. Of course, I had no sibling's to grow up with."

"Must have been lonely."

"It was. From the picture you sent, your daughters look like you with your dark hair."

"That's all they got from me. The rest is their mother. They have her green eyes and her smile." He shifted position and stared straight ahead.

"I'm sorry, I didn't mean to bring back bad memories."

"What makes you think they are bad memories?"

His voice betrayed the hurt he felt and something more. Guilt maybe.

"Because you're not smiling."

"I don't smile at everything, but you're right. I was thinking of the day their mother was killed." His gaze narrowed. "It was my fault."

"Mrs. Black told me it was a terrible accident."

"I shouldn't have let her ride him. She wasn't skilled enough to handle the big black."

Hearing this gave her a niggle of worry. "I hope you don't harbor resentments which will keep me from riding. I'm very well trained and used to riding a mount with some spirit."

"No." He shook his head. "Absolutely not. You won't be riding. At all."

Unable to believe her ears, Bella turned to him.

"Are you saying that because your wife

was killed while riding, you won't allow me to do so? Even when I assure you I am very skilled? I can prove it to you. There is not a horse alive that I cannot ride."

Alex's jaw was set. "No, no riding."

He acted like that was the end of the matter, but Bella had another outcome in mind.

"That's idiotic. Your wife was obviously not the skilled horsewoman I am. I've been riding since I was a girl, and I don't intend to stop now. If I have the time, I would like to ride."

"The only time you'll ride a horse is if I'm alongside of you and that's not likely to happen. Too much work for each of us to do."

In her haste to escape Sydney Rockwell, she might have been selfish. Alex expected certain things from her and she couldn't provide them. "You might as well know now, I can't cook. Well, that's not entirely true. I have one meal I cook and do very well. That's all. One meal. Beef stew and I can make the lightest bread you've ever eaten."

"Figures. A woman with your looks wouldn't know how to cook. But doesn't matter. I'll have Cookie teach you."

"Who is Cookie? Your trail cook?"

"One and the same. He's the cook when we take the cattle to market. We have to drive them to Bozeman and the railroad there."

"Who cooks for you now?"

"Martha Jennings."

"Why can't she continue to cook for you?"

"Because I have a wife now who is supposed to do three things. Raise my girls." He ticked off one finger. "Cook." He ticked off the second finger. "And lastly clean. Those are the three things you need to do. That's all."

"What about being your wife, is that to be in name only?"

"Yes."

"What? No, that can't be."

"Why? I thought you would be happy that I wouldn't be claiming my husbandly rights."

"Keep your voice down."

She cocked her head in Jack B's direction before panic seized her. She had to get him to change his mind.

"But you have to, at least once. The

marriage has to be consummated to be legal."

"Maybe. We'll see."

Bella looked at him and saw by the clench of his jaw and the white knuckles on the reins, his mind was made up. Well, she'd just have to change it. She couldn't be a virgin at this time tomorrow. She just couldn't be.

CHAPTER 4

The beautiful country they traveled through probably would have seemed more so if she hadn't been so worried about the coming night's activities. Even with that weighing on her mind, what she saw was breathtaking. Tall, snow-capped mountains stood to the north and west. To the east and south spread prairie which, when the snow melted, would be full of green grass, and according to the book she read about Montana Territory, would be fine for grazing cattle. In her mind's eye she imagined the prairie full of grasses and flowers she'd never seen before.

The trees were covered in frost and snow, and she didn't think at this late time of the day the temperature would get high enough to make any change. The countryside looked like a winter wonderland and, despite the freezing temperature, she was awestruck by the vision around her.

"What are you thinking so hard about?"

She looked over at Alex, who appeared to be watching her.

"I was just thinking how beautiful it is here, and how wonderful it will be in summer. You can take the girls and me on a picnic and we can all relax as a family." *I remember the last picnic I'd been on. Benjamin had taken me to Central Park. He'd tried to kiss me and I rebuffed him. He never called again.*

Alex smiled. "I'm glad you're thinking of us as a family. That kind of thinking bodes well for our future."

"Of course, I do. You and your daughters, Rose and Violet, correct?"

"Yes, that's right. They're named after my wife's favorite flowers."

Bella let that go. She wouldn't get into an argument over the children's names, just because he was thinking of his dead wife.

"Well, you are my family and now I'm a part of yours…if you let me be."

He furrowed his brows. "What's that

supposed to mean?"

Bella took a deep breath and looked at her lap, then up at him.

"It means you need to start thinking of me as your wife. Your previous wife is dead, and sad as that is, I'm your wife now."

"Of course, you are. Have I said differently?"

Actually he hadn't, but the mention of his former wife as though he was still married to her, was disconcerting, at the least.

"No. Not really. You've introduced me as your wife to the one person we've met, which was Miss Effie at the restaurant. But you referred to the girl's being named after *your wife's* favorite flowers. She is your late wife"

"And Effie will have it all over town I've remarried. Don't be surprised if you get a few visitors come to inspect you."

"I'll welcome them to our home." *Maybe we'll be friends. I'd like to finally have friends of my own and not those of my mother.*

"Good. Miss Effie was right, Jo Longworth, the sheriff's wife, and Clare Donovan, wife of one of the mine owners, will definitely want to meet you. They came from the same agency you did. Sam and Jesse are very happy with their wives, which is why I used that company."

"I am hopeful we will have the same outcome. Do they have children?"

Maggie's comment about her success rate with marriages seems to be true. At least in Hope's Crossing, she was 100 percent right...so far.

"Sam and Jo have one son and Clare and Jesse are expecting a child next month."

"How wonderful."

"I suppose."

"You don't think it's wonderful they obviously fell in love with each other, the baby being a product of that love?"

"You don't have to be in love to make babies, though in these cases, it's true. They did fall in love. Great for them, but don't you be getting your hopes up. I loved once and then I killed her."

"You didn't kill her. A fall from a horse killed her. She was obviously not skilled enough to be riding the horse she chose."

His eyes flared as if lightning was shooting through them. "You don't know. You weren't there. I might as well have smitten her with my own hand."

She reached her hand underneath the blanket to rest on his knee. "You didn't, Alex. *You did not kill her* and you need to accept that and move on."

"I can't. I know what I did."

I have to help him get past this before our marriage has any chance. "Did you bring the horse out for her to ride?

"No."

"Did you saddle it for her? Did you refuse to ride with her?"

"No. She didn't ask. I didn't know she was going riding or I would have stopped her."

"Exactly. She did all of that on her own. There was nothing you could have done."

Alex was quiet for several moments as the wagon rolled along.

"I can't get over the fact it was my job to protect her and I didn't."

"What could you do? She didn't tell you and I would guess that was on purpose. She knew you would say 'no' and she wanted to ride."

"We're almost home."

She let the change of topic go. Alex was obviously uncomfortable talking about his late wife's accident.

He pointed toward the buildings in the distance.

The one she could definitely make out was the barn. Big and red, it stood out from the others. As they drew closer she saw several buildings stood grouped together, all painted white. The house was two stories with a large porch that wrapped around the two sides she could see.

Another, smaller house, only one story, stood across the yard from the big house. In between the main house and the barn was another building, one story, at least twice as long as it was wide. Next to the house were several small structures and one that was very short as well.

"What are all the buildings? I see at least two houses and what, according to the book I read on Montana Territory, must be a barn."

"Very good. There is the main house, it's the two-story one with the large porch, then there's my foreman's house. The other buildings are the chicken coop, pump house, ice house, smoke house, outhouse and back towards the barn is the bunkhouse and another outhouse for the hired hands. There are ten men…eleven now with Jack B."

"Did I hear my name?"

Jack B sat up, stretched and yawned.

"I needed that nap. I haven't stretched out to sleep since we left Cheyenne."

"Your special long bed awaits you."

Alex smiled and explained. "When Jack B was here for the second season, I had a bed made special. It's long enough for him to stretch out without hanging off the end. All the men know not to claim that cot, because it belongs to Jack B.

"That was awfully nice of you," said Bella. *He's very generous. I value that in a man. I don't want a miserly husband.*

"I keep hoping Jack B will stay on with us permanent and not just half the year."

"I meant to tell ya, boss. If you still want me I'll be stayin' on."

"That's great Jack B. Glad to have you."

Alex smiled, clearly pleased.

"Who is watching the girls while you came to get us in town?" asked Bella. She gazed around at all the buildings. She'd have to learn what each one was for. With so many, that could prove to be a daunting task.

"Martha. You'll get to meet her and you can ask her if she'll teach you how to cook."

"Wonderful." She couldn't garner any enthusiasm for that particular chore.

Alex pulled up to the side of the house. He set the brake, jumped down, and came around to help Bella down from the wagon.

Jack B took his saddle and saddle bags and he headed toward the bunkhouse.

Alex grabbed her bags from the back and led her up the steps, across the covered porch to the side door.

Outside this door was a long table with towels and three basins. She thought they must be for the help to wash up before going in for meals.

He entered the kitchen and called to Martha.

"We're home."

"No need to bellow, I'm right here."

Bella held out her hand and went to greet the woman wearing a flowered apron. She was a handsome woman, about fifty with blonde hair that was starting to show gray. "You must be Martha Jennings. Alex has told me how much he appreciates your help."

Martha straightened and smiled wide.

"Well, that makes me feel right special. I was afraid he took me for granted."

"Oh, not at all. He couldn't handle his daughters and this ranch without your assistance. He's very aware of that. Before we go any farther, I'd like to ask you a question." It was time she asserted herself

"Go right on ahead. You got my attention."

"To be honest, I can't cook. I never had to learn how. Beef stew and bread are all I can make. I wonder if you'd teach me, or tell me of someone who might have the time and be willing."

"Well, I've got my own husband to take care of, but I can help you out. I've been meaning to tell Alex." Martha looked over at him. "You know Poppy Montgomery? Her husband was killed in that cave-in at the Johnson mine last year."

"Yes." He'd set her valises on the floor and now leaned against the door frame with his arms crossed over his chest. "I'm familiar with the cave-in taking a man's life."

"Well, Poppy's been trying to make a living taking in laundry, but it's not going so well, and I think she'd be amenable to coming to work for you permanent like."

Bella turned to Alex and put her hand on

his arm. "Oh, that would be wonderful. To have someone here who could help me and teach me what to do. I could concentrate more on the girls." She leaned in and whispered, "I'll pay for her to work here, just please let her come."

Alex frowned and said out of the side of his mouth. "I can pay for a housekeeper. You can keep your money." Then he spoke louder, "and speaking of my daughters, where are they?"

"I didn't mean to insult you. I simply have no idea what your finances happen to be," whispered Bella.

"They're out back making a snowman," said Martha, pointing over her shoulder.

At that moment, two little girls, bundled up with wool coats, knit scarves, hats and gloves ran through the door, racing each other toward their father.

"Daddy!" they shouted together as they crashed into his legs.

Alex laughed, bent down and picked up one girl in each arm.

"Rose." He looked at the little girl in his left arm who wore pink hat, scarf and gloves. "And Violet" he said to the little girl on his right who was in blue. "This is your new mama. Can you both say hello?"

"Hello," they said together.

Bella put her hand on his arm. "I think it's a good idea for you to call me Bella. When you feel ready you can call me Mama, but until then Bella will do."

Rose smiled and so did Violet.

"See, I tole you she'd be nice. Daddy wouldn't bring home no mean lady," said Rose.

Alex chuckled and set down both girls.

"You two can go back to making your snowman or come in for the rest of the day. What do you want to do?"

They put their heads together and chatted for a few seconds. Then Rose, the girl in pink, looked at her father. "We be out there."

"All right. But when you are called in, you will not whine to stay out longer. Do we understand each other?"

"Yes, Daddy," they both nodded vigorously and said together, then ran back through the door from whence they came.

"They're lovely."

"They're wild. I hope you can tame them," said Martha.

"They're still lovely."

"I tend to think so, but I'm a little biased. Come on we'll get you settled."

Bella liked what she'd seen of the house so far. They'd entered directly into a foyer in front of the stairs. To the right was the parlor which was decorated with chintz curtains and lace doilies on the end tables. The sofa was a lovely blue floral brocade. There was a leather wing chair on each end of the couch.

"Do you still plan on putting me in the guest room?" she said when they were out of earshot of Martha, who Bella thought went back to the kitchen.

"Yes. For now."

"But, I thought—"

With an arm around her waist, he brought her close and whispered in her ear. "There won't be any consummating of this marriage tonight and I don't want to discuss the matter any further."

"We'll see," Bella said under her breath. She had to get him to make love to her. Her marriage may be a sham but she would be protected if it was consummated.

Alex led the way up the stairs, carrying her bags.

"There are four bedrooms up here. The

girls share one here on the left, though the one across the hall is actually theirs as well. They just seem to use only the one for the most part."

He opened the door to the room on the left, which looked like it had been hit by a hurricane. Clothes and toys were everywhere.

Bella's hand flew to her throat. "Oh, my goodness."

"We quit trying to keep it neat. They just tear it up again."

Alex closed the door.

"The room across from theirs has a bed and the rest of the furniture but they prefer to be together."

They came to the two bedrooms at the end of the hall.

"My bedroom is on the right, yours is here."

He opened the door to a pleasant room.

An iron bedstead with colorful quilt on it was set against one wall. Light coming through the gingham curtains added a cheery glow to the room. A dresser, bureau and wardrobe all made out of a light colored wood were varnished for a high sheen.

"It's lovely," Bella said flatly. Her closet

in New York was as big as this room, but still it was a perfectly acceptable for a guest room, but she wasn't a guest. She wanted to be a wife.

"You needn't be so disappointed. I don't understand you. Most women would be glad I don't do my husbandly duty."

Bella's eyes opened wide. "Duty. That's right it's your duty to take my virginity. You must do your husbandly duty."

Alex lifted his eyebrows and widened his eyes, looking at her like she was a lunatic and maybe she was, but she knew staying a virgin could cost her her life, because she would rather die than let Sydney Rockwell touch her.

CHAPTER 5

Alex set her bags just inside the door to the room and walked across the hall.

"This is my room."

He opened the door on the largest of the four bedrooms.

Her room was the smallest. Maybe that meant she wouldn't be staying in it for very long. His room had all the same furniture as the other rooms, with the addition of a nightstand on either side of the biggest bed she'd ever seen and a vanity under the window.

The size of the bed made sense. Alex was a big, tall man and a regular bed would not have been very comfortable.

"Did you have this made the same time

you got Jack B's bed? It's got to be a special order like his was."

Alex put his thumbs in his pockets and leaned back on his heels.

"Yup. Got a deal having them both done at the same time. I was tired of being wedged in those little short beds."

"I can imagine."

"I'll leave you to unpack your bags. Then it will be time to start dinner. I don't know what Martha has planned. Tomorrow, you can make your beef stew. You need to make enough for fifteen people, and remember that twelve of those people are hungry working men, so you'll need a couple of pots of stew and lots of bread, too."

"I'll remember." *Normally I make a batch to feed me and the staff back home which was seven people. I figure if I triple the recipe and the amount of bread I bake, I should have enough to feed all those people.*

"You'll have to check with Martha to see if we have everything you need for the dish."

Bella unpacked her valises and put things away. Just in case he didn't move her into his room. Maybe this was best. She could go to his room for their intimate relations and then come back here to sleep. He probably would prefer it that way, anyhow.

She looked over her clothes. She had one pink seersucker dress, one gray wool dress, one blue serge skirt, three white poplin shirtwaists, one black bombazine skirt, that she used to garden in with a pink shirtwaist, a purple silk dress with black lace trim and her dark red riding outfit but based on what she'd seen they were all still much too elaborate. Most had lace or ruffles or both except the riding suit. Well, perhaps the town had a seamstress who would have enough time and the patterns to make her some plainer dresses, skirts and blouses. Her mother had been right about the boots though. Her riding boots had been more than adequate for walking the dusty streets and over the dirt and whatever else was on the floor of the way-stations where the stage had stopped.

When she'd finished putting away her clothes, she found her way back to the kitchen. Martha was there, preparing dinner.

"Can I help?"

She watched Martha scoop the juices

from under a roast and spoon them over the top before putting it back in the oven.

"You can peel those potatoes."

She jutted her chin toward a large bowl heaping with potatoes.

"All right. I know how to peel vegetables for when I make my stew. Alex says we will have that tomorrow, if we have the ingredients. Do you have stew meat or steak I can cut up?"

"We do. There's ten pounds of stew meat in the icebox. Onions, carrots and potatoes are in the root cellar."

"Good, I'll get it ready tonight and then it can simmer all day tomorrow. The stew will be good and thick by dinner time."

Martha crossed her arms over her chest and then took one hand and rested her chin on it. "How is it you can make beef stew and bread and nothing else?"

"It's my favorite meal. Beef stew isn't considered gourmet enough for my father, so the only time I got the dish was when I made it for the staff. It was my joy. I actually like to cook, but only on rare occasions did I get the chance."

"Well, you'll have plenty of occasions to cook now. Every day, three meals a day.

That should keep you busy."

Bella frowned and shook her head. "I'll do my best, but how am I supposed to devote the time the girls need if I'm cooking all the time?"

"Plus, you have to milk the cows and gather the eggs before breakfast."

Alex's deep voice cut through the air like a hot knife through butter, reverberating through her. It didn't matter what he said, she liked hearing his voice.

"Milk chickens and gather cows?" She shook her head, not believing her ears. "What did you say?"

Alex chortled.

"Do you know how to milk *cows* or gather eggs from the *chickens*?"

"No, I don't. You might as well ask me to milk a chicken, which makes as much sense."

"We'll have to see to your education."

Martha waved her spoon at Alex. "First, she's helping me in the kitchen. Then you can see to her other educational needs."

He held his hands up. "All right. I know when I'm not wanted."

He turned and left.

Bella peeled all the potatoes in the bowl

and then cut them into chunks for cooking. *Already I'm a terrible wife. I can't cook, I don't know how to do the tasks Alex wants me to do. And now I'll be a bad mother because I can't be with the girls like I should be.*

Martha spooned more of the meat juice over the roast.

"What are you doing, Martha?"

"I'm basting the roast. It helps the meat brown and keeps the outside moist."

"How long do you cook the roast?"

"For a roast this size, about three hours. The boys like their meat a little on the rare side, so I cook the beef for about fifteen minutes per pound."

"What else are we having for dinner tonight?" She looked around and saw bowls on the counter that would be filled with mashed potatoes and whatever else they were having, a platter for the roast. The bread was already out on two plates waiting to be cut.

"First, we're having supper. Around here, dinner is at noon."

"Really, that's good to know."

"I have two quarts each of green beans and sweet corn I canned last summer as well as fresh bread and butter. Then I also made two yellow cakes with chocolate icing for dessert."

"Sounds like a lot of food to me."

"Cowhands are hard-working men and they eat a lot. You better get used to cooking more food than you can imagine. If you think you have enough add half again as much. They will go back for seconds and thirds if the food it available. You will never have leftovers."

Martha turned the roasting pan so another side was toward the fire box.

Bella knew enough to know that was so each side browned equally and the roast cooked evenly.

"Let's set the table. Everyone eats here, in the kitchen. We have a dining room we use for holidays and such, but for every day, we just eat in here. Sixteen of us will be present today."

Bella set the huge table, big enough to hold twenty people. Each side of the table had two five-foot long benches and one chair at each end.

When the food was done, Martha put it all in big bowls and on platters. Two bowls or platters of each dish, one at either end of the table, so everyone could reach the food and load their plates.

Alex sat at the end of the table with one daughter on either side.

The girls sat in special-made high chairs so they could eat at the table.

"You sit in the chair at the other end. You're the missus and that's your seat."

Bella sat where she was directed and ate her first meal with her new family. The men didn't speak for the first half of the meal, then, when they'd gotten a little food inside them, they opened up, teasing each other and talking about their day.

She sat there and took in all the commotion, reveling in the liveliness of the meal and wondering how in the world she'd ever remember their names. Back home, her family never had meals like this. Instead, theirs were where you were not to speak while eating unless the occasion was a dinner party.

When they were done eating the cowboys got up one by one and left the table. She and Martha cleared the table and Martha washed the dishes while Bella dried. She then put them away, with Martha's help, learning where all of them went. Alex took the girls upstairs and readied them for bed.

After all that was complete, Bella was exhausted. The travel, the new people, the wedding, everything was coming down on her and she needed to rest before she collapsed.

"Excuse me," she said to Alex and Martha in the parlor after supper. "I'm turning in a little early tonight. The traveling, the wedding, all of it has just worn me out." The ring on her finger is a foreign weight, one she'll have to get used to just as she'll have to get used to the rest of being a ranch wife, but she'll learn. The learning will just take some time.

She gave a little laugh and went over to Alex.

"May I have a goodnight kiss, husband?"

Alex stood and kissed her proffered cheek. She wished he'd grasp her by the waist and kiss her deeply, but that would be unseemly in front of Martha.

"Goodnight, Bella."

"Goodnight, Alex. Martha."

"Goodnight, Bella," said Martha with a wave. "I'm going home now."

"Do you live far?"

Martha laughed. "No. Just over the hill. Take me about ten minutes to ride home."

"It's awful cold out, sure you don't want to stay?" asked Bella.

"No. I'm fine." Martha turned to Alex. "Think on what I said about Poppy Montgomery. The situation would be a good one for both of you."

"I will go talk to her tomorrow," said Alex.

"Good. Glad to hear it. Now, I'll take my leave."

Martha left the parlor with Bella and went toward the kitchen while Bella went up the stairs.

When she reached her room Bella thought about the seducing she was supposed to do, so her husband would get rid of her pesky virginity, and decided she could stay a virgin for another night.

*****

"Get up, sleepyhead."

She heard the deep voice in the back of her mind and ignored it, too tired to get out of bed.

"Come on now, Bella. Cows need to be milked and eggs gathered. Then you have to cook breakfast."

"Go away. It's too early. It's not even light outside yet."

She turned her back on Alex and the lamp he held.

The next thing she knew, the blankets were at her feet and he slapped her on the bottom.

"Get up."

"All right. Go away so I can get dressed."

"My pleasure, but if you don't get up and get dressed then I will come back and dress you myself."

"Your warning is accepted."

She sat up and put her feet on the floor, which was freezing. Bella dressed with all haste in her gray wool dress. She'd worn it when she visited the kitchens of the church and helped to feed the poor.

The delicious smell of coffee emanated from the kitchen and got stronger the closer she got. By the time she reached her destination, her mouth was watering.

"Coffee. Thank goodness."

She went to the cupboard and grabbed a cup, thankful Martha had her put the dishes away last night so she wasn't opening all the cupboards this morning, just to find a cup.

"I'm glad to see you're wearing a heavy dress," said Alex.

"I brought the plainest, sturdiest clothes I had."

"Well, I wouldn't exactly call it plain with all that lace and those ruffles on the skirt, but it'll do."

Bella looked down at her dress and wondered what he would think of the others she'd brought with her. This one was the most modest. Oh, well, it was what is was and she'd deal with that tomorrow. She put on her coat, hat, scarf and gloves.

"I'm ready. Let's go milk some chickens."

She grinned at Alex.

He laughed and shook his head.

"You're quite the surprise, Mrs. Hastings."

"Glad I can keep you on your toes, Mr. Hastings."

He grabbed a towel wet it in the warm water still heating on the stove and put it in the milk bucket. Then they walked out to the barn, the lantern in Alex's hand lighting the way. Inside Alex took the lantern from the wall, lit it and handed it to Bella.

He walked to the first stall.

"This is Flower."

"Flower?" Bella giggled softly.

"We let the girls name the milk cows."

He grabbed a small stool from the end of the stall and sat it near the back end of the cow.

"Sit here."

She sat.

He squatted next to her, put a shallow pan under the cow and leaned on her side with his cheek.

"Lean in and wash the udder with the towel you brought," he explained as he did it. "Then after that…" He put the towel on his leg. "Punch the udders gently to get the milk flowing. We are imitating the movements of a calf nursing and a young one would nudge the udder to start the milk just like this."

Bella watched him intently.

"Now take a teat and squeeze and pull, squeeze and pull." He leaned back. "Now you try it."

She laid her cheek on the side of the cow like he had and took hold of a teat. Then she squeezed and pulled. Nothing.

"What happened? Is she empty?"

He chuckled. "Not hardly. You're

worried about hurting her. Don't be. Squeeze and pull hard. You need to get that milk out of her or she'll be in pain."

Bella frowned. "She will?"

"Yes. Her udders fill with milk every day and she keeps making milk even if you don't take it. They will get too full and she'll hurt and leak, just like a woman would. So, to keep her from having pain, we pretend we're her calf, and we milk her every day. So squeeze and pull hard."

Bella did as he said, and she got a squirt of milk. By this time the barn cats and a bunch of the kittens had gathered.

"Give them a squirt or two."

"What?"

She pulled her head away from Flower's side.

"Squirt the cats. Bend the teat and aim at the cats. They love it. When you've got a little more milk in the pan, we'll give it to them and then we'll take the rest of the good milk in the pail. The first few squirts have to be discarded, anyway. We don't want milk that's been sitting in the teat or the first squirts that might not be as good as the rest. The cats love it, so it's a win-win situation."

"I'll have to remember that. Can I have a

kitten?"

"I suppose so. Why would you want one in the house when you have all these out here?"

"I've always wanted one but Father never would let me have a pet of any kind."

"All right. Are you comfortable doing the milking? Because you'll be doing this on your own. I have to take care of the horses while you milk the cows."

"I've got this, go care for the horses."

He smiled.

"You'll do," he muttered as he stood.

Minutes later, she finished with Flower and moved on to the next cow.

"What is this one's name," she called to Alex who was down at the other end of the barn forking hay into the horses' stalls. This cow and the last one both were white with black patches of hair.

"Tree"

"Tree? How old were your daughters when they named these cows?"

He laughed. "One. They were just learning to talk."

"Now that makes sense."

She finished with the second cow and stood, putting her hands to the small of her back.

Alex walked up to her as he brushed hay from his pants and coat.

"Can I have that kitten now?" Her heart pounded a rapid tattoo. She'd finally have a pet.

"Sure. Go pick one out."

He pointed to the back stall.

"You know if I let you have one, the girls will want one as well?"

They walked back to the last stall.

"Probably, in which case you can bring them down here and let them pick out their own kitten." As she walked down the aisle between the stalls she couldn't help but notice how well kept the barn was. The outside of the building was freshly painted but she hadn't expected the inside to be painted at all, but it was. The stall gates were all painted the same red as the outside of the building. She liked it, liked there was pride of ownership evident for all to see.

"Up until now I've been telling them 'no' urging them to visit the kittens in the barn."

Bella understood having three cats in the house would probably be more difficult than he would like.

"Would you rather I came to visit the kittens, too? It's all right if you do, I understand."

"No, you can have your kitten and when they get theirs you'll have three you have to take care of."

"We'll tell the girls they have to take care of their kittens even when they get big and if they don't want to do that, they can come visit the kittens in the barn."

"They'll just say they will and for the first few weeks, they'll care for them dutifully. Then they'll forget and you'll have to take over."

She shrugged. "Well, I'll be feeding my kitten anyway, so it won't matter." Three cats. Hopefully they won't be a lot of work, but what did she know. This was her first pet.

"As long as you know what you're in for."

"I have the chance to make friends with your daughters and I'm taking it. We'll see how it works out."

CHAPTER 6

Bella chose a little yellow tiger stripe kitten.

Alex told her it was already about twelve weeks old, but was a runt and probably wouldn't be very big.

"That's wonderful. That way, I'll always have a kitten."

Alex shook his head and picked up the milk buckets.

She put her kitten inside her coat and carried the lantern while they trudged toward the house. Once inside, Bella put the kitten on the floor where it meowed pitifully.

"He misses his brothers and sisters." Alex set the milk buckets on the counter and then leaned against it.

"He'll have a couple as soon as the girls have breakfast. Do you have a box I can put him in?"

"I'll empty the wood box. That should work for now, and then I'll make a bigger box for him and his siblings to live in."

He's helping me to bond with his girls. "Thank you. That's very nice of you, considering you don't want the cats in the first place."

"Never let it be said I stand in the way of your relationship with my daughters. You need one, and I know that. I'll help you in whatever way I can."

"That's so nice of you."

"So, now that the cat is taken care of, we need to gather the eggs from the chickens. I've got three dozen laying hens. Each gives us one egg per day, which barely gets us through breakfast for fifteen people."

She tapped a finger on her chin. "That doesn't leave any for baking. Have you thought of getting more chickens?"

"I've thought about it, but until you came we didn't need them for more than breakfast."

"Well, now you do. You can either get

more chickens or start buying two dozen eggs every week. That's only three extra eggs a day."

"You think you'll need that many more?"

"Probably. Some weeks, anyway. If I bake a dessert or two every day, I'll easily use that many extra eggs. It would be easier if we had Poppy already here. She could give us a better idea of what will be needed for baking. Speaking of which, you'll have to move me into your room when Poppy comes."

"Why? She can take the other spare room."

"Look," she said hands on her hips. "Maybe you don't care what people say about you and about our marriage, but I do. I don't want them to know you find me so abhorrent you can't even sleep in the same room. Which may be the case, but I'd rather other people didn't know."

He frowned. "What would make you think I find you anything less than pleasing to look at?"

"You refuse to sleep with me, or to bed me. I never thought I was beautiful, but I didn't think I was ugly either."

"You're not ugly. You're beautiful, that's why I can't have you sleep with me. I couldn't keep my hands off of you"

"Then we wouldn't be at cross purposes. I want you to make love to me and you want to, so what's the problem?"

"I'm not ready to make love to another woman. My wife—"

She sighed, trying to be gentle. "Your late wife is dead. It's time for you to live again."

"I…I…don't know how."

She walked over to him, ran the back of her hand down his face, and cupped his jaw. Then she snaked her other hand around the back of his neck to bring his head down to hers.

"Let's learn together," she whispered before she kissed him.

He was stiff for a moment or two then he melted and put his arms around her back, bringing her close, deepening the kiss, making her knees weak.

When they broke apart, both were breathing heavily, trying to catch their breath.

"That was pretty…nice." Bella smiled as she turned away.

"Nice!? I'd say that was pretty darn good."

"Maybe, but I think we can do better if we have more practice. After all you're the first man I've ever kissed."

His eyes widened and then he let his eyelids go to half open. "The first...and the only."

He lowered his head again and this time took her lips, then pushed his tongue against her closed mouth, she opened and he pressed his advantage. Tasting her, playing with her, dueling with her. When he pulled back this time, she could barely breathe much less talk.

After a few moments, she looked up and found her arms wrapped around his neck. "Well, when did that happen?" She started to ease them away, but he shook his head.

"I like your arms just where they are. I like your body flush with mine. To feel you against me."

His voice vibrated through her, the deep sound touching her soul.

"Good, because I like to feel you, too. Don't be afraid of me, please. Make love to me."

"Let's start with you sleeping in my

room when Poppy comes."

"When will she be here?"

"I'll go get her today, if she's willing."

"Oh, I hope she is."

He was weakening. She could feel it and knew he would make love to her soon and she'd be safe.

"I have to go to work now. Today, I'll get the eggs. You get the girls up and dressed."

He released her.

At the loss of his touch she felt bereft. Being in his arms is where she's supposed to be, where she belonged.

Bella didn't waste any time. She went upstairs and packed her clothes back in her valises. She might be moving today, but she wasn't taking the chance of having Alex upset with her moving too soon, so she'd wait until he gave the okay. But until then, she'd live out of her luggage.

After she was done repacking, she went to wake up the girls.

Both of the little ones were in the single bed together, unwilling even in sleep to be parted.

Bella sat on the bed and looked down at their dark little heads facing each other.

She pulled back the blanket and smoothed her hand over first one cheek and then the other.

"Wake up sweetings. Time to get up."

They slowly opened their eyes and yawned.

"Do we have to get up? We're tired, ain't that right, Rose?"

"Uh huh. Tired." Rose turned away and pulled up the blanket.

"Come on sleepyheads. Time to get the day started. What do you want for breakfast today?"

"Scrambled eggs," said Violet.

"Oatmeal," said Rose.

"One or the other. Decide."

They put their little heads together and then Rose answered. "I guess we'll have eggs this mornin'."

"Okay. I figure I should be able to scramble some eggs. How hard can it be?"

She discovered the task wasn't hard at all and made a mental note to have scrambled eggs every morning.

Today, she scrambled all the eggs she found in the icebox and that Alex brought inside, in two large skillets. In a third skillet, she laid strips of bacon to fry. This cooking stuff wasn't all that hard. Of course, this was just breakfast, the easiest meal, but she wouldn't say that to anyone.

Before the men came in, she remembered the wash basins on the porch and prepared them with hot water. She made sure there was soap and towels.

The men ate everything she prepared and she knew by the looks on their faces they could have eaten more. She made a another mental note to cook twice as much of everything and to have Alex buy a dozen more laying hens.

Today she'd bake bread for tonight's dinner, er, supper. *I must remember it's supper not dinner. Dinner is lunch. So confusing.* She'd bake eight loaves of bread that should cover those two meals. For dinner, she was hopeful Poppy would be there and able to help her.

After breakfast she made sure the girls were occupied with their dolls before she started on the bread. She got the dough prepared, separated it into two big bowls and covered them with dish towels to rise.

Then she got her kitten, which was sleeping in the box Alex gave her after she'd given the little thing a saucer of milk. Next she went in search of the girls and found them playing in the parlor.

"Rose, Violet, I have someone I'd like you to meet. This is Maddie, my kitten."

"Oh, can I hold her?" they said together in high-pitched voices.

"Me first," said Rose.

"No, me first," said Violet.

"Girls. Girls."

Bella got on her knees and held the kitten.

"I want you both to learn to be gentle. For now, I want you to just pet the kitten."

They did and their movements were a little rough.

Bella lifted Maddie out of their reach.

"Slowly. Gently. Like this."

She showed them how to pet Maddie, how to scratch under her chin and behind her ears. They learned very quickly and soon, Bella put down the kitten and let them play with her. Bella had found a piece of string and showed them how to play with Maddie by pulling the string along the floor and holding it up for her to bat at.

"Can you two, watch Maddie while I go back to the kitchen and prepare the bread?"

"Yes, ma'am, Bella," said Violet.

"We'll take good care of her, won't we Vi?" said Rose.

Vi shook her head up and down vigorously. "We'll take good care of her."

"Yup, we will," agreed Rose.

"All right, you know where I am. I trust you to be careful with her."

Bella went down the hall to the kitchen and punched down the dough and let it rise again. Then she did the dishes from the morning's breakfast and started to prepare her stew. In the icebox, there was a mountain of steaks as well as her meat. She took the ten pounds of beef cut into cubes, browned it and split it evenly between two large Dutch ovens. She then added big chunks of carrots and covered it all with water and then brought the stews up to a boil before moving the pots to the back of the stove to simmer. The onions and potatoes would cook faster than the beef and carrots. She'd add them later so they didn't turn to mush.

She went to the parlor to check on the girls and found them dressing the kitten in doll clothes.

"No. Rose, Violet. The kitten is not a doll. Don't dress her up, she doesn't like it."

Bella rescued the kitten and removed the clothes.

"You two go to your room and don't come out until I call you to dinner."

"You can't tell us what to do," said Violet. "You're not our mama."

"I am your mama now. You don't have to call me mama, but you do have to mind me. Now you stay in your room and remember how to not play with the kitten."

They looked up at her. Violet was mutinous and Rose had tears in her eyes. Bella almost backed down and let them come back to the parlor to play, but she remained strong and watched them, hang dog expressions on their faces, as they walked up the stairs to their room. Bella followed them to make sure they went. Then she walked out of the girls' room and down to the kitchen, all the while petting the kitten and trying to calm her.

"I'm sorry, little one. I should have known they were too young to have a kitten. I guess their daddy does know best."

Bella heard Alex's boots in the hall.

"I'm glad to hear you say that."

Alex walked in with a brown-haired woman in her fifties following behind him.

"I was talking to my kitten. The girls were dressing her in doll clothes."

Alex chuckled. "I'm sure the kitten—"

"Her name is Maddie."

"Just so you know, Maddie is a boy kitten."

She lifted the kitten and looked in his face. "Oh, well, I guess Maddie could be a boy's name."

"Anyway." He moved to the side and let the woman come into the kitchen. "This is Poppy Montgomery. She's agreed to become our cook and housekeeper."

Bella put Maddie in the box by the stove where she...he could keep warm. Then she walked over to the middle-aged woman with gray in her brown air. She was only a little shorter than Bella.

"I'm so happy to meet you and thrilled you've come to help us. I barely know my way around a kitchen, but I want to learn, and the girls are already a hand full."

"I'm very happy to be here, Mrs. Hastings."

"Call me Bella, please."

"And I'm Poppy. Now if you'll show me to my room, I'll set my bags down and we can get started on dinner."

"I'll take your bags up, Poppy," said Alex. "You can stay here and help Bella. The men will be starving when they come in. Breakfast was somewhat spare this morning."

"I cooked all the eggs and bacon we had, but I didn't fix anything else." *What I wouldn't give for Marco's bakery where I could order the croissant's and sweet rolls I would need for this crew.*

Poppy looked around the kitchen, and saw the pots on the stove. She went over and looked inside. "Well, we'll make sure there is plenty of food for dinner and I see you have supper started. Fine beef stew and fresh bread. I'll whip us up a couple of cobblers and we'll call supper good. Now for dinner let's look in the ice box and see what we've got."

Poppy took over the kitchen.

Bella was perfectly happy to let her. Next, Bella finished kneading and shaping the dough and put it into eight bread pans for the final rising before baking.

At the same time Poppy cut fifteen steaks into strips and fried them and then made gravy. She found jars of green beans with bacon and potatoes in the root cellar and several quarts of apples and peaches.

While the bread was baking, Poppy mixed together the crust for the cobblers, made three instead of two and planned one for dinner. They were set, and when the men came in and saw all the food, they cheered.

They were quick to assure Bella breakfast had been fine but they were glad more food was served for dinner.

Bella laughed. "I thank you all for being so kind. I've a lot to learn. The first thing being you all have good appetites. Now that Poppy is here, we'll see you get full."

After they all ate, Bella and Poppy cleaned up.

Alex came in and took Bella aside.

"You should move your things out of the guest room. I set Poppy's bags inside the door and then I emptied a drawer in my bureau and moved my clothes to make room for yours in the closet."

"Thank you. I'll move them immediately?"

Narrowing his gaze, he shook his head. "Don't make more of this than it is. I still haven't changed my mind. Or maybe a better way to put it is I haven't decided what to do with you. Yet."

"I see." Moments later Bella got her already-packed valises and unpacked them in Alex's bedroom.

Alex came in while she was putting away the clothes. He shut the door and came up behind her. He ran his hands up and down her arms and then turned her so she faced him.

"Why do you make this so hard for me?"

Before she could answer, his lips crashed down on hers and he kissed her like he hadn't before. So thoroughly her knees shook when he finally broke the kiss.

"Alex," she breathed.

"Bella, I want you, more than you can imagine."

"Then take me. Make me your wife. Now."

"I can't. I've work to do, but I will." He drew a hand down his face. "I don't seem to have much choice where you are concerned."

Inside she shouted for joy. "I'm glad to hear that."

"I'm not. I don't want to need you. To need to be in you. To have you under me and…"

"Oh, please keep talking. What? What

do you need from me?"

He set her away.

"Things I can't ask of you."

She cupped his face. Her pulse raced and her breath barely made it out of her throat.

"You can ask anything of me. If it's in my power, I'll give it to you."

"You don't know what you're saying."

"Then show me what I don't know."

Again, his lips claimed hers and he backed her toward the bed.

CHAPTER 7

Bella hung on to Alex, taking what he was offering and walking with him to the bed. She wanted this. She needed this. And it scared the hell out of her.

Alex broke away after they reached the bed and gently lowered her onto the mattress.

"Are you sure, Bella?"

"I'm sure. If you never want to make love to me again, that's fine, but I want this marriage consummated. The deed is important."

Alex continued to kiss her and then he slowed as if something bothered him.

"Why is it so important? Why do you need the marriage consummated? Everyone will think we have whether we have or not, so why is it so important?"

Alex sat on the bed next to her.

She sat up.

"I can't be a virgin."

He lifted his eyebrows. "Why? Who will know?"

"I'll know. He'll know."

"He?"

Her shoulders slumped and she picked at a fold in her skirt so she wouldn't have to look at him. "I suppose I should tell you everything. You can't exactly throw me back, now can you? The reason I became a mail-order bride is that my father sold me to one of his business associates. Or, actually, he sold my virginity and if Sydney Rockwell finds me…I can't have it. He won't want me if I'm not a virgin."

Alex narrowed his eyes and clenched his fists. "How would he know? You'll tell him, but how will he be sure? He can't unless he takes you."

Her body stiffened and her back was ramrod straight. "He'll have to kill me. If he doesn't believe me and wants to test the theory, he'll have to kill me, because I won't ever let him touch me."

He grabbed her arms. "Will he be coming for you? Have you put my children in danger?"

She shook her head. "They aren't in danger. He only wants me. And if he happens to find me here, which I doubt, I will go quietly, so the girls are not in jeopardy. I would never have agreed to be your wife, if I thought I was putting any of you at risk."

Alex furrowed his brows and waved his hand. "And I'm supposed to just stand by and let this happen? Let some man take my wife?"

Guilt assuaged her. She should have told him before they married, but she was too scared. "Only if he finds me. In all likelihood he won't. I covered my tracks pretty well."

"But it's a possibility?"

"Yes, I suppose it is."

Alex stood and paced in front of the bed where she sat.

"How can you just assume you've covered your tracks or no one is threatened except you?"

"My mother helped me escape by telling my father I was sick with chickenpox and he had to stay away for two weeks."

He shook his fist in the air. "I can't believe you're so naïve. This Rockwell person will want you no matter what. You're a beautiful woman and that's what he sees, not just your virginity. That may be part of the reason he gave your father, but I can guarantee he'll want you, regardless."

What he right? Was she naïve? Oh, God. Her shoulders slumped. "Then I need to leave. I never wanted to put anyone else in danger."

"You can't leave you're my wife."

She looked up at him. "We haven't consummated our vows. You can get an annulment."

"I don't want a damn annulment."

He stopped and pulled her to her feet. His lips smashed hard against hers. She tasted the coppery tang of blood, but she gave all that she had to the kiss.

He pulled back but kept his hands clamped on her upper arms.

"You're my wife. For now. For always. I won't let any lecherous, son-of-a-bitch take you away."

"Alex, I'm sorry. Truly, I never thought I was putting anyone else in harm's way."

"No, you just thought to use me, or someone like me, to take your virginity and then what, go back to your rich little girl's life?"

She'd been so selfish, never taking into account his feelings. Her eyes filled with tears but she wouldn't let them fall. "No! I never intended on going back. I'm here to stay. I take my vows seriously and I already love the girls. They grabbed my heart as soon as I met them. I would never knowingly hurt them or allow anyone else to hurt them."

She wrenched herself free from his hands and rubbed her arms where he'd held her.

"I never would have come if I, for even one second… Never."

Alex ran his hands through his hair.

"I don't know what to do with you."

"Send me away if you believe I would intentionally hurt you or the girls in any way."

"I can't. You're my wife. You're not the only one who takes their vows seriously."

Saddened by the reality of the situation, she said, "Your choice is an annulment. It's the only way you can be safe. If you won't file for it, I will."

He fisted his hands. "You won't. You're my wife. And whether I take your virginity or not, I won't let you say I'm any less than a man."

She gasped. "I'm not saying that...never would I say that."

"If you get an annulment you're saying just that. He's not man enough to consummate this marriage, so I want someone who will do it."

She shook her head. "No. That's ridiculous. No one would ever think you are less than a man."

"Except apparently my wife who wants an annulment. Well, you won't get one, and this time tomorrow you won't be able to file for one. Tonight I'm making you mine."

Alex turned on his heel and left the room.

Bella collapsed on the bed. She'd never had such an argument with anyone in her life and for it to be Alex, her husband, that she had the fight with...she shook her head, trying to clear it.

"Well, that went well," she said to no one.

*****

That night at supper Alex tapped his knife on his cup for attention.

"I want all of you to be armed at all times. Don't go without your guns for any reason. Men may be coming to do Bella harm. We can't let that happen. Report if you see anyone unknown. Any stranger at all, male or female you report it to me."

All of the men started talking at once.

"Quiet! Quiet everyone."

The men slowly quieted.

"Bella do you have anything you'd like to say to these men?"

She swallowed hard and stood, her hands clasped in front of her.

"I'm sorry. To each and every one of you, I'm so very sorry. My intent in coming here was never to put you, or anyone else, at risk."

"Ah, that's okay, Bella. We know you wouldn't try to hurt us on purpose," said Jack B.

"No, Jack B, I surely wouldn't. I've only been here a few days and already you are all my family. I would never hurt any of you."

She looked down the table to Alex.

His gaze was focused on her.

"Ever." She didn't look away…couldn't

look away if she'd wanted to.

"Daddy." Rose pulled on his shirt sleeve. "Does me and Vi have to carry our slingshots, too?"

Alex finally broke the link and looked down at his daughter.

"No, sweetheart. You and Vi are safe. Daddy will always keep you safe."

Bella's heart broke. How could she have thought no danger existed to anyone but herself? How could she be so selfish?

Later after the girls were in bed, Bella went to Alex's bedroom and prepared for bed. She took down her hair, sat at the vanity and brushed it thoroughly before putting on her nightgown.

Alex came in while she was brushing it, and latched the door behind him.

"What if the girls need something in the night?" she asked, jutting her chin at the latch on the door.

"They'll knock and we'll get clothes on before we open the door."

She gathered her hair and began to braid it in one single plait.

"Leave it down. I want to see you with your hair down."

"Fine. Will you turn your back so I can

get in my night clothes?"

"There are no night clothes for us. Keep a robe at the bottom of the bed in case the girls wake us in the night. But, you and I do not now, nor will we ever, wear nightclothes."

"But, but…"

He walked over to where she sat at the vanity and put his hands on her shoulders. He squeezed gently and massaged her with his thumbs.

"Nothing will be between us."

She looked at him in the mirror, standing behind her and slowly shook her head. "Everything is between us. You'll never trust me now."

"Take off your clothes, Bella. We'll discuss this in bed."

Bella bowed her head and looked down at the table with spots for creams and jars. "No. I'll be naked and I don't mean just without clothes."

"I won't hurt you, Bella, but I am giving you what you wanted. Tonight I'm making you my wife."

She looked back at him in the mirror. "I don't want you to do it in anger."

"I'm not angry. I should be, but I'm not.

I know you did what you thought was best at the time and you wouldn't hurt the girls for anything."

"That's true. I care for the girls."

She also loved the feel of his hands on her, rubbing her, up and down her arms. The way his hands came around her neck, his thumbs pressing into her back and shoulders. Bella didn't want him to stop.

He leaned down and whispered in her ear. "Come with me, Bella. Come now."

She stood and let him lead her to the bed.

His hands moved from the magic he was working to unbuttoning her dress, allowing it to fall to the floor. Next he unhooked her corset and it fell on top of the dress in a heap.

She only had her chemise and bloomers to cover her now. She wanted to grab them tight but knew he wouldn't allow it.

He tugged at the tapes holding up her bloomers and the bow opened. He pulled the tapes out at the sides until they were loose and the garment shimmied down her hips, over her thighs, adding to the pile on the floor.

Her chemise was the only thing between

her and being totally naked. She shivered but whether from the lack of heat in the room or from nervousness she couldn't tell. She always hated being naked, doing so is a show of trust for her. Alex was not just baring her but her heart and she wanted his heart in return. How could she feel so close to him and yet so far away at the same time? How could he not feel this...thing between them?

Alex unbuttoned his shirt and took it off, then his pants. He still had on his longhandles until he unbuttoned and stepped out of them, as well.

He was naked as the day he was born, and he was amazing. His body was hard lines and sharp angles compared to her soft and curvy one.

He reached out and pulled the ribbon on her chemise, undoing the bow and the garment fell open revealing her to him.

He slid the chemise off her shoulders, down her arms and off her body. Bella wanted to run for cover but he kept her pinned in place with his gaze.

"You are beautiful."

His gaze traveled up and down her body and then up again to lock with her gaze.

"Turn down the covers and lie on the bed."

She did as he asked, unable to refuse him, his voice mesmerized her.

Alex sat next to her. His hands traveled up and down her legs, over her mound and up her stomach to her breasts. There he stopped the travel and concentrated on massaging first one and then the other, pinching her nipples lightly until they stood up.

Then he lowered his head and took one of her nipples in his mouth. He suckled her.

She fisted her hands in the sheet, while every nerve ending she had in her body came alive.

"What are you doing to me?" she panted.

"I'm making love to you. I'm preparing you to take me inside."

Alex continued his ministrations and Bella loved every movement he made as she reached nearer and nearer some pinnacle she couldn't see.

Finally, she couldn't stand it anymore.

"Alex, please. Help me."

He pressed his hand on her mound and put his finger down and tapped a part of her, she'd sometimes felt when she rode Champion. But this was ever so much more intense. The little tap...tap...tap was all she needed. When next she was coherent, she realized she'd seen the stars. No, not seen them, she'd been one, shooting through them to the final explosion.

Alex soothed her. Kissed her and suckled her.

Then her breathing came back to normal, and he smiled.

"My turn."

He rose above her and placed himself at her opening. With small movements he entered and stopped shortly when he reached her barrier.

"This will hurt. Not a lot, but some."

He kissed her, tasted her, sucked her tongue into his mouth as he plunged forward.

The pain was sharp and then faded to just an ache.

He stopped as soon as she gasped.

"Bella. Are you all right?"

She didn't answer, waiting to hear what her body said.

"Bella?"

His voice sounded strained.

"Yes, I'm fine. I'm all right."

"Thank God."

He moved inside of her, his gaze never leaving her face. It was like he watched her for any signs of discomfort.

She had none, so she smiled. The fires were building within her again.

"Faster, Alex. Faster."

He greeted her request with a smile.

"Yes, ma'am"

After a bit, he pounded hard into her, once, twice and then again. Finally he groaned and buried his face in her neck muting her name.

He lay heavy upon her. Even though his was a great weight, she didn't mind. She relished it and put her arms around him before urging him to raise his head.

"Kiss me."

He lifted his head and his blue-eyed gaze locked with her brown-eyed one, before he lowered his head to press his lips softly against hers. Nibbling, tasting but in no hurry.

Then he rolled off her and to his side of the bed, taking her with him. He tucked her against his chest.

"You're mine now, Mrs. Hastings. Now

and forever."

"And you're mine, Mr. Hastings. Forever and a day."

"Sleep now," he said immediately falling into slumber.

But she couldn't sleep. She kept going through all the scenarios that could happen if Sydney Rockwell found her. Of him kidnapping the girls or her. *Please God if he comes, let him take only me.*

Bella needed to be able to shoot a gun. If she was here alone with just Poppy and the girls, she wanted to know that she could protect them.

Tomorrow, she would broach the subject with Alex. Surely, he could teach her or maybe have one of the other men do it.

Tomorrow, she'd know.

*****

That morning after breakfast she approached him. "Alex, can I talk to you? Privately."

"Sure. Let's go to the parlor."

When they arrived, she sat on the sofa and he in one of the Queen Anne chairs next to it.

Bella couldn't stay seated. She got up and paced in front of the chairs and sofa.

"What did you want to talk to me about? I have work to get done."

"I want you to teach me to shoot a gun," she blurted out.

With his elbows resting on the arms of the chair, he steepled his hands. "Why?"

"Why? In case someone comes to harm us. What if I'm alone with the girls and Poppy? I need to be able to take care of us."

"I have men protecting you and I am protecting you. You don't need to learn."

"I do. What if you're not here or what if—"

"That won't happen. Leave it be."

He turned and walked from the parlor.

"Well, heck." Bella said after he left. "We'll just see about that."

CHAPTER 8

June 16, 1874

Sydney Rockwell reviewed the report from his Pinkerton detective. They'd found Isabella in a small mining town in Montana Territory called Hope's Crossing. Now that he knew where she was, he had to decide if he wanted to go there to get her or have her brought to him. How anxious was he to have her?

He decided he'd waited this long, a little longer wouldn't matter. After walking to his outer office, he spoke to his secretary.

"Mrs. Gregson, please send for Mr. Williams and Mr. Jones."

"Yes, sir, Mr. Rockwell."

He didn't know their real names. He called them Williams and Jones and they didn't correct him. These men were the ones he summoned whenever he needed something enforced, like the gambling debt owed by Ernst Latham. They also took care of his special needs. Things a Pinkerton detective wouldn't normally do.

At this point, knowing Bella had married, receiving the gift of her virginity was no longer feasible, but he would have her regardless. He didn't have to marry her now. He could keep her on the side and no one could complain, since Ernst had been silenced.

Williams and Jones arrived at his office approximately thirty minutes after the messenger was sent.

"Sit down, gentlemen."

He pointed to two brown leather chairs in front of his desk.

"I have a job for the two of you. I want you to bring back my stolen bride."

"That shouldn't be a problem," said the one in the gray suit.

"Normally, I would agree with you, Mr. Williams," said Sydney.

"What is the problem then, Mr.

Rockwell?" asked the man in the brown suit.

"Unfortunately, my bride took it upon herself to marry someone else, Mr. Jones, and that someone, Alex Hastings, must be eliminated before I can reclaim her."

"That's a special assignment and will cost you more," said Mr. Williams with a sidelong glance at Mr. Jones.

"A lot more," said Mr. Jones, nodding to Mr. Williams. "Plus expenses."

"I'm well aware of the cost." Rockwell heaved himself out of the huge black leather chair behind the desk. "And I will pay you double that cost when you get back here with my bride."

"Half up front, Mr. Rockwell, as usual."

"Certainly. You'll each find five thousand dollars in the envelopes on the desk in front of you. Another five thousand will be waiting when you return with my bride, Isabella."

"Where is your bride now?"

"In a place called Hope's Crossing in the Montana Territory. The trip to get there will take you approximately two weeks. I suggest you leave with all haste."

Misters Williams and Jones stood. Each pocketed the envelope from the desk without looking inside to count the money.

"We shall see you again in approximately one month's time," said Mr. Jones as he and Mr. Williams turned to leave the office. "Would you like to be notified when the deed is done?"

"Yes, I wish to know when Mrs. Hastings is indeed a widow and back to being Miss Latham."

The men nodded and left the office without another word.

Sydney walked to the window of his fifth floor office. No office in the city was higher than his. A new building was being built down the street that would be ten stories. He was tempted to move his business there just so no one could look down at his office...down at him, but common sense prevailed and he decided it did not matter.

Now, he just needed to occupy himself until he heard back from Misters Williams and Jones. He sat back at his desk and looked over the ledgers of people who owed him money. Some of their services may come in handy when Isabella is back under his control.

*****

June 15, 1874

Bella had been at the ranch for more than three months, now. All seemed to be going well, though Alex still kept her at arm's length. He refused to be anything other than civil except when they were in bed. There he acted like he loved her and he made love to her on a nightly basis.

But she couldn't crack his shell. He was closed off. Refusing to love her, refusing to give her his heart as she had given hers to him. She tried to show him she loved him by the little things she did...like taking him his dinner when he was working in the barn. Making love to him rather than letting him make love to her.

He'd also refused to teach her how to shoot a gun. But she kept after him. The skill was important and she knew it, even if he didn't believe her.

The girls were different. They had just turned four when she arrived on March 1st and they loved her. Neither of them spared their love always giving her kisses and hugs. And she loved them back. They might as well have sprung from her loins for the love she had for them was so great.

On this day, Poppy was in the kitchen with Bella who was learning how to bake cookies.

"My grandfather used to make what he called tea cakes," said Poppy. "They are basically a sugar cookie."

"How do you make them?"

"Well you start with one cup lard and one cup sugar. Cream them together, add three eggs, one teaspoon of vanilla extract and beat all that together well."

Poppy took those ingredients and showed Bella how to beat them together until they were creamy.

"Then, take one half teaspoon salt, three cups flour and one teaspoon each of baking soda and cream of tartar. Mix all of those ingredients together into dough. Roll it out to about one quarter to one half-inch thick and cut it with an empty can. They make nice sized cookies. Bake them in a hot oven until very, very lightly browned, that way they stay soft and don't get crunchy like a regular cookie."

Bella wrote down the recipe as Poppy did all of the actions. The smell of the cookies brought two little girls to the kitchen.

"Whatcha doin'?" asked Vi.

"You makin' cookies?" asked Rose.

"Can we have some?" asked Vi.

"Oh, yes, please can we have some?" said Rose.

Bella smiled at their enthusiasm. "Yes, I'm learning to make cookies and yes, you can each have one with a glass of milk." She moved to the counter, took some of the dough and began rolling it out.

"Yay!" they shouted together.

"Whoa," said Alex as he came into the kitchen from outside. "What is so good?"

"Mama said we can have a cookie and milk," said Rose.

"Yup, she did," said Vi.

Bella nearly dropped the rolling pin in her hand. Mama. They had called her Mama.

She looked up at Alex with tears in her eyes.

He smiled down at her.

"Mama, huh?" he said to the girls.

"Uh huh, iffn' Bella don't mind," said Rose. "Me and Vi would like to call her Mama."

Bella dropped to her knees and took one of her daughters in each arm.

"Nothing in this world would make me

happier."

"Good. Can we have two cookies?"

Bella laughed.

Alex chuckled.

"We'll compromise. You can each have one and one half cookies."

"Yay!" They cheered again.

Poppy shook her head and smiled at the little girls.

"They've got you wrapped around their little fingers."

"Yes, I guess they do. They certainly have my heart."

"You spoil them," said Alex, standing in the doorway to the hall.

"They deserve to be spoiled a little. It's just half a cookie and look how happy they are. Speaking of being spoiled a little, will you spoil me and teach me how to use a gun, please, Alex?"

Alex sighed and ran his hand behind his neck. "You've been after me for weeks and I guess you've worn me down. I'll teach you. We'll start tomorrow after breakfast."

Bella ran to him, threw her arms around his waist and hugged him.

"Thank you."

She looked up at him and was pleased to

find he was smiling. Then he put his arms around her and kissed the top of her head.

"Maybe I should have taught you before."

*****

Morning came, and Bella hurried through her chores, and eating breakfast. Finally, it was time. She took off her apron and put it on the kitchen counter, grabbed her coat and went to find Alex.

It may be June but he air had a bit of a chill and until the sun rose over the mountains and warmed the air it would be cold. The start of another beautiful June day in Montana Territory.

She found him in the barn.

He looked up when she came in. "Good. Let's get started. First you're learning how to load and unload the weapon."

He showed her the unloaded cylinder with chambers for six bullets. He quickly filled each chamber with ammunition and snapped the cylinder into place. Then he opened it up again and removed each bullet by pushing them out with a small ejector rod attached to the underside of the barrel.

"Now you do it."

He handed her the unloaded gun, and she did everything he did.

"Very good. You didn't miss a step."

Bella smiled broadly, pleased with his praise.

"Now, reload the pistol and let's teach you how to shoot it."

She did and, when it was ready, she looked up at Alex.

"What now?"

"Come with me. I've set up some cans to use as targets."

They walked out of the barn and beyond the corrals to an open field where she saw six cans set on stumps of wood.

"Let me show you how it's done. When you're shooting, you need to cock the gun by pulling back on the hammer, and then gently ease the trigger back. Don't pull it quickly, you'll lose your aim and miss whatever you were shooting at, whether a four-legged varmint or a two-legged one."

He took the gun, aimed and fired six times, hitting each can, and knocking it off the piece of wood.

Alex walked out to the targets and set them up again.

"Now you try it."

She nodded and took the pistol. Bella reloaded it and had to hold it up with both hands, because the weapon was too heavy for her to use just one. She aimed down the barrel to the sight and then to the can beyond. Then she cocked the gun and had to aim all over again. Finally satisfied, she eased back on the trigger like Alex taught her. The recoil brought the gun up and back, forcing her to aim and re-aim several times after each shot.

The first shot she fired she missed the can and hit the wood. The second shot went wide left and hit the ground between the two targets. So it went for each shot. She reloaded and followed the process again. And again. And again.

Finally, when she'd hit half of the cans in one round, Alex let her stop.

"You'll have to practice every day. I'll reload the shells every night so you can."

She was so tired she could barely lift the gun to hand it to Alex, butt first.

"Thank you. I never realized shooting would be so difficult, or so tiring."

"More to it than just point and shoot if you want to hit anything, especially what, or who, you're shooting at."

"Well, I definitely want to hit what I'm shooting at."

"Yes, you do. Especially if it's a man trying to hurt you."

Shivers went up and down her spine. *Or someone taking me away from my family.*

"Yes, especially then. I guess I'd better go help Poppy with dinner, or at least take the girls off of her hands."

She tried to smile, but the effort was weak.

"I don't expect you to ever have to use this weapon, but it is good to know you can if you need to."

"Yes, I hope I never have to use it either. It's too darn heavy."

Alex laughed.

"They should have smaller models made just for women."

"They do. I can special order you one or Joe Stewart, the local gunsmith, might have one already made."

"You will do that?"

She looked up at him as they walked through the barn, headed to the house.

"Yes, I will."

"That would be wonderful. Then I can put it in the pocket of my apron and carry it with me."

Alex stopped and gazed down at her.

"You really are frightened aren't you?"

"If they've been looking for me now would be the time for them to start showing up. And I've been thinking about what you said and I think it wasn't just my virginity Sydney Rockwell wanted."

"I've tried to tell you that."

"I know. But I won't let him take me. I'll never voluntarily leave my daughters or you."

His gaze softened. "You really do love the girls, don't you?"

"Yes. They are my daughters. You heard them call me Mama." She swiped a tear away with her fingers. "They are my daughters, now and forever."

Alex wrapped her in his arms.

"Nothing sweeter you could say to me, than you love my daughters."

He lowered his head.

She lifted hers.

His lips touched hers, gentle, and not what she wanted. She needed fierce. She needed her warrior.

She cupped his jaws with her hands and held his face while she deepened the kiss.

Bella opened her mouth and dueled with his tongue. She tasted him, coffee and his mint toothpowder. Around her were all the smells of the barn, the hay, the straw, the animals, yet his was the only scent that registered. A potent mixture of sandalwood and man.

Alex picked her up so her feet swung about eight inches off the ground and carried her to the stall filled with fresh hay. Then he set her on the floor and raised his head.

"Take your coat off and spread it on the hay."

She did as he requested.

"Now remove your bloomers and lie down."

She did and watched him as he readied himself for her.

He came down over her and then as he loved her, he reached between them, touched her, and she flew to the stars.

Alex cried out her name, collapsed on top of her, and then rolled to his side, winded.

After a bit, when she'd caught her breath, she smiled at her husband.

"Well, that was nice. Can I expect that kind of ending to our shooting practice every day? If so, I'll bring a blanket to lie upon."

Alex chuckled.

"That might not be a bad idea. I can't seem to keep my hands off you, no matter how much I try."

"Why would you try? I'm your wife and I don't want you to keep your hands off me. I want more children, Alex."

He sat up abruptly beside her, then stood and fastened his clothes.

"Put your clothes on, and let's go to the house."

His voice was like ice. How could he go from being in the throes of passion and then become so cold?

A knot grabbed her stomach. "What did I say wrong? That I want children? Or are you afraid you're falling in love with me?"

"I'm not afraid I love you. I don't. I can't. I still love Kate. I'll always love Kate."

Bella gasped and furrowed her brows. "I see."

"I never meant to hurt you, Bella. Truly. I—"

He did say he wanted a marriage, in name only. "No, it's fine. I know you lost her in an accident. I guess I thought you'd moved on because you married again."

Resignation filled his voice and he ran his hand through his hair.

"I married again so the girls would have a mother. I thought you understood that."

"That doesn't preclude having more children."

"It does for me."

Sadness filled her. She'd always thought she'd have two or three more babies to join the girls. "Where does that leave us? At some point in time I'm bound to get pregnant."

"Unless we stop having sex."

She winced. "I prefer to think of it as making love, but I guess having sex is more accurate."

"Bella."

She turned away and headed back to the house. Tears rolled unchecked down her cheeks.

I thought I'd been making headway, tearing down the wall he has around his heart. I was wrong.

CHAPTER 9

On Wednesday, July 1st, Alex came in from outside and announced they were going to town on Friday.

Bella looked up from washing the dishes and grabbed a towel to dry her hands. "Why are we going early?"

"Because Saturday, is the Fourth of July and there is a party at the Donovan's we are attending. So I need to do Saturday's chores, including getting our weekly supplies, a day early."

She threw the towel on the counter. "You could give me a little more warning when we're attending parties. What if I didn't have a dress that's appropriate?"

"This is Hope's Crossing, not New York City. Your best dress will be fancier than anything the other wives are wearing."

She sighed and wrung her hands together. "Perhaps, I shouldn't wear it, then. I don't want to seem out of place."

Alex walked up behind her and put his hands on her shoulders, slowly massaging them and her neck.

"I want you to wear your best dress. It's that purple one isn't it? I haven't seen you wear that one yet."

"I'm surprised you noticed. I was saving it for a special occasion."

"You don't have that many dresses and this party is the perfect time for you to wear it."

She leaned back against him, craving his touch. Since their interlude in the barn two weeks ago, Alex hadn't so much as kissed her.

"I suppose it is. Will I meet more of your friends there?"

"Yes. You've met the ones that matter. The Donovan's and the Longworth's. There will be several other couples there, but I don't know them as well as Jesse and Sam. And plan on staying overnight at the hotel. Poppy will watch the girls for us."

He wrapped his arms around her waist.

She laid her hands on top of his arms, totally relaxing into him. "It'll be fun to stay at the hotel, to have a night just to ourselves."

He kissed the side of her neck.

She bent her neck giving him better access.

He kissed her again, then ran his tongue over the area his lips had just been.

Her breathing grew shallow and she wanted nothing more than to turn in his arms and kiss him fully, but she also didn't want to scare him away. Didn't want him to remember why he'd quit touching her.

As though he could read her thoughts, his hands froze and he lifted his lips from her neck. Then his hands fell away.

She was again bereft.

She'd started wearing her nightgown to bed since Alex didn't want to touch her anyway. Now that she knew he missed her as much as she did him, she was going back to sleeping in the nude. Perhaps he'd wake her some night and make love to her after all. Oh, he'd regret it the next morning, but she wouldn't.

Perhaps, if they got on better terms, she'd tell him she thought she was already pregnant. She hadn't had her flow since coming to Hope's Crossing, so she was fairly sure. And if she was expecting, he could start making love to her again, but she wanted him to come to that conclusion without him knowing she was with child.

She estimated she was about two months along. Soon, she'd start to show and she couldn't keep the news from him, so she had to work on him before that. Yes, cuddling with her naked body ought to do the trick. She hoped.

That night she got ready for the bed and hung her robe over the footboard as usual, but she forwent the nightrail. Instead, she slipped under the covers before Alex came to bed and feigned sleep when he got in next to her.

She heard him curse softly under his breath. But then he lay back and she rolled over and cuddled with him as she always did. She loved the feel of the warmth of his skin on hers.

Soon he was touching her and kissing her. Waking her body with sensation.

"Alex…"

"You know what you do to me."

His tone was accusatory but he didn't

stop touching her. He didn't stop from rolling her onto her back and coming over her and entering her.

It didn't stop her soft cry of pleasure.

After they were both complete, they lay tangled in each other's arms.

"I should be angry," he said after. "But I can't be, not when it's my fault, I can't resist you."

"I don't want you to resist me. I love having you make love to me."

"But the children that we could—"

She placed her fingers over his lips.

"Not could. I'm think we have already made a child."

He stilled.

"Are you sure?"

"Yes, I'm pretty sure." *My breasts have been tender and coupled with no monthly flow, yes, I'd say I'm sure.*

"Then there is no need for us to abstain."

He kissed her, turned her on to her back and loved her again.

*****

Mr. Williams and Mr. Jones arrived in Hope's Crossing on Wednesday, July 1st and checked into the Hope's Crossing hotel.

As they signed the guest register, Effie

Smith watched them intently. They seemed too well dressed to be miners, both wearing nice three-piece suits and bowler hats, with neatly trimmed hair and mustaches.

"You boys here to mine gold?"

"No, ma'am," answered Mr. Williams.

"Doin' some huntin' while you're here?"

"Not really, ma'am," said Mr. Jones. "Actually, you might be able to help us. We're looking for the Hastings' place. We've got business to discuss with Mr. and Mrs. Hastings."

"You're in luck. They'll be in on Saturday, for the Fourth of July celebration, so you can talk to them then."

"Thank you, Miss…" said Mr. Jones.

"Smith. Effie Smith."

"Thank you, Miss Smith. Your information is very helpful."

Effie smiled.

"You're welcome, gentlemen. Here are the keys to your rooms."

The men left the front desk and climbed the stairs.

As soon as they were out of sight, Effie scribbled a quick note.

"George," she called.

A young man with brown hair thick with curls came out of the dining room.

"Yes, Miss Effie."

"I want you to take this note to Alex Hastings out at his ranch. Now hurry, boy. Get your horse and ride."

She handed him the note and then looked up the stairs making sure the men weren't watching.

Alex needed to be prepared for these two. Danger was written all over them.

*****

A knock sounded at the front door.

Vi and Rose ran toward it. "We'll get it," they shouted together as they opened the door.

"Hello," said a male voice.

Bella came forward. "Hello, George. What are you doing way out here?"

"Miss Effie sent this note for Mr. Hastings."

He held out a piece of paper.

"Come in George. You must be tired after your ride. I have some coffee and freshly baked cookies you can have. Keep Vi and Rose company while I go to the barn and get Alex would you please?"

"Sure."

"Vi. Rose. Take George to the kitchen. He'll help you to get milk and cookies. Show him where everything is."

She watched the three of them go and then left out the door toward the barn. As she walked she read the note.

Alex,

Two men arrived looking for you. They don't look like they are miners or ranchers, but rather city slickers. I didn't tell them where you live, though I did tell them you'd be in town on Saturday. Thought you should be aware.

Effie

Bella gasped and her heart pounded in her chest. She was sure these were men sent by either her father or, more likely, by Sydney Rockwell. She ran to the barn. When she arrived, she didn't see Alex anywhere.

"Alex?"

"Up here."

She looked up and saw him at the edge of the loft.

"What brings you out here?"

"Come down, please. George is here. Effie sent him out with this note."

Alex descended the ladder that was

attached to the loft floor and walked over to her.

She handed him the note and then wrung her hands.

"They're here."

Alex read the missive and then looked up.

"Certainly sounds like it. We'll see if they are who we think they are on Friday when we go in for supplies. They won't be expecting us a day earlier than Effie mentioned, and we can observe them."

"If they're looking for me, they'll have a description of what I look like and there's not enough women in Hope's Crossing for them to be confused or think me anyone but who I am."

"Maybe you shouldn't go."

She straightened. "No. I want to know what they look like as well and tell them to go back where they came from. That I'm married now and Sydney Rockwell no longer has any say so about what I do."

He squared his shoulders and jutted out his chin. "I'll meet with them alone."

"But Alex, I need to—"

"No." He took her by the shoulders. "You need to be safe."

She thought about his words and decided maybe he was right. Besides, depending on where he met them, she could watch from afar.

"Where will you meet them?"

"At the hotel."

Alex paced in front of her to the loft's ladder and back again.

"Where do you want me to be?"

"With Sam and Jo. You can't be any safer than with the sheriff and his wife. Both Jo and Sam used to be bounty hunters and I'm betting that's what these men are, in a sense."

"I hate that you want me to be so far away. I need to recognize these men." She frowned and narrowed her eyes. "What do you mean…in a sense?"

"From Effie's description of them as 'city slickers' they don't appear to be dressed like any bounty hunter I've ever seen. I think they were sent directly from New York by your *betrothed*."

She fisted her hands. "Don't call that vile man that."

He tilted his head. "Really? Did you not hear the sarcasm?"

"I'm sorry. I'm just worried."

143

"You're carrying your gun, aren't you?"

"Yes." She patted her pocket. "Always."

"Good."

Friday couldn't come soon enough for Bella. She needed to know who these men were and what they wanted with her and Alex, even though she was afraid she already knew.

Wednesday night, after receiving the note from Effie, Bella had tossed and turned so much she was afraid she'd awake Alex so she finally got up and went to the parlor to read.

Alex found her asleep in the chair hours later and carried her upstairs to bed which was where she was when morning came.

She rose from the bed and dressed quickly in her gray wool dress. Poppy had helped her raise the hem at the back so the material didn't drag the ground without the small bustle which she no longer wore.

Milking the cows she talked to them like they were real people just like she always did.

"Hello, Flower."

She petted the side of the cow then set down the milking stool.

"What am I going to do? I need to know

what these men look like. I need to know who to avoid and who to shoot on sight."

"You're not shooting anyone on sight, even if you know what they look like."

She jumped and looked up at Alex, who was holding a pitch fork.

"But—"

"No buts. You're not committing murder."

"I wouldn't shoot to kill him."

"Then why shoot at all? If you're firing that gun, it should be to kill."

"Why not just wound him? Shoot him in the knee or something?"

Alex's voice rose and he opened his arms wide. "Because he can still shoot you and the only way you can assure that won't happen is if you kill him first."

Alex took off his hat and ran his hand through his hair. Frustration emanated from him.

"All right. Don't get so worked up. "

She walked over to him, wrapped her arms around his waist and leaned into him.

"I promise if I fire that gun I keep in my pocket, it will be with the intent to kill whatever I'm shooting at."

"Good. I don't want to have to worry

about you and our child, too."

"You don't need to. I'll be very careful for both of us." She leaned back and placed her hand on her belly. When her clothes were off, she was beginning to show. But with them on, no one would have any idea she was increasing.

He gazed down at her and raised her chin with his knuckle. Without saying another word, he leaned down and took her lips with his in a blazing kiss.

She wrapped her arms around his neck and kissed him back. Bella pressed forward with her tongue.

He smiled through the kiss and opened.

When they broke away from each other, Bella, breathless as usual, smiled up at him.

"You always take my breath away."

"As you do mine."

"That must mean something. Maybe we are good for each other."

He stiffened just a bit.

"All it means is we lust after each other." His voice was flat.

"Just lust?"

"Just lust."

Bella backed out of Alex's arms, not wanting to touch him. Her pride hurt that he would think they had nothing special between them.

"I should let you get back to work. I just wanted to show you the note."

"Bella."

Shaking her head she turned away.

"I have work to do."

"Bella, I—"

"I'll see you at dinner."

She picked up the milk bucket and walked back up to the house without looking back. Didn't want him to see the tears that streaked down her cheeks.

CHAPTER 10

Friday, July 3, 1874

Friday morning came. She and Alex lay together after making love and before they needed to get up for the day. Cuddled into his side, her head resting on his chest, was the way she wished she could always be.

"Shall we take the girls with us? They enjoy playing with little Paul and they've been very good lately, maybe they can get a candy stick at the mercantile?"

Alex chuckled.

"You just want to reward them for finally calling you Mama."

Bella closed her eyes and then looked up and grinned. "Well, maybe a little."

Alex threw his head back as far as the pillow would let him and laughed. When he sobered he said, "I would love to take the girls, but not this time. Not with men in town that may want to do you or me harm."

"You're right. I should have remembered. This is not one of our regular trips is it? We have an ulterior motive."

Alex squeezed her shoulder.

"We'll take them next time."

"Sure." Bella wondered if there would be a next time. What if these men took her away from the people she'd come to love? But what choice would she have if they threatened to hurt any of them? None. She would have to go with the men and it terrified her.

"Bella. Bella!"

Alex snapped his fingers in front of her face.

"Yes? What?" She shook her head to clear the visions there.

"You were awfully far away from here, just now. What are you thinking about?"

"Nothing. It was nothing."

He tilted his head and looked at her.

"It was not *nothing*. You were thinking about him weren't you? Rockwell?"

"Yes. I can't help but wonder, if these men are his hirelings, what they would do to take me back?"

"I think the question we should be asking is 'what won't we do' to stop them. Depending on what leverage they use, you or I would do whatever they ask."

"I know. I'm scared, Alex. What if in coming after me, they take the girls? I couldn't bear it if I was the cause of injury to them. Maybe you should just let me go."

"Never. You carry my child."

"Is that the only reason?"

"It's the only reason that matters."

She looked up into his eyes and wondered how he could not know he was shredding her heart. Bella closed her eyes to keep from crying. She wanted, no needed, for him to love her. Her heart ached. That did not appear to be something that would ever happen. She moved away from him and they both got out of bed and dressed for the day.

They did not discuss the subject again but went about as though the incident had never happened.

Bella dressed in a dark blue dress with lace on the top of the cuffs only. It was very plain and non-descript. Something that wouldn't stand out in anyone's mind. She still hoped to get a look at the men. Tomorrow she would wear her purple dress like she and Alex agreed.

They arrived in town after a long quiet ride. They had said nothing to each other. That was until they arrived at the Longworth's home.

Alex knocked.

Jo answered the door. "Come in. To what do we owe the pleasure?"

Alex ushered Bella across the threshold. "I'd like for Bella to stay here while I go meet some people."

Bella shook her head. "I'm not staying here. I have as much or more invested in seeing them than you do."

"You need to stay out of sight."

She crossed her arms. "They'll see me anyway. All they have to do is watch you until I join you again and they'll know. Why not just get it over with?"

"She has a point, Alex," said Jo Longworth.

"See," said Bella. "And Jo was a bounty hunter for many years before she married Sam."

"If it were me," Jo continued. "I'd just hang around town until I saw you two together. Then I'd devise a plan to get you apart. Come in to the kitchen and sit down. We can discuss this over coffee."

"You're not helping, Jo," Alex said through gritted teeth as he followed her.

Jo turned and lifted an eyebrow. "Alex, if you really believe these people are bounty hunters then you'd better listen to one of the best in the business, and that was me."

"She's right," said Sam, as he walked into the kitchen holding his baby son, Paul, in his arms. "If you like, I'll go with you. If necessary, I can ask the men to move on."

"All that will do is put them out of our sight, and we won't know where they are or when they might attack, so to speak," said Alex as he sat at the table with Bella and Jo.

"You think these men are here to hurt you?" asked Jo.

"You might as well know since we've brought it to your doorstep," said Bella. "I became a mail-order bride to escape a marriage that was being forced on me by my father. He lost money to a man named Sydney Rockwell and to settle the debt he…he sold me to him."

Jo put her hand over her mouth. "Oh, my God. How could he do that to his own flesh and blood?"

"I don't know, but I will never forgive him. I was lucky and found Alex, but now it looks like Rockwell has found me. Effie sent a note saying two city-slickers arrived in town asking after Alex and me. That can only mean one thing. He found me." Needing some comfort, Bella held her arms out to Paul and the baby leaned toward her.

Sam passed his son to Bella then sat across the table from Alex. "When you tell them you're married and to go back home, I take it you think they won't do just that."

"No, I think they will have orders to make me go with them. That's why two men are here. I'm afraid if I don't they'll hurt Alex or the girls." Her stomach roiled and threatened to give up her last meal.

"Why would you think that?" asked Jo. She got up to get the coffee for them.

"Because Sydney Rockwell is a vile, loathsome bastard, who thinks the law is for everyone except him." Bella bounced Paul gently on her hip and then talked to him. "Isn't that right, Paul? He's a mean, evil, depraved, excuse for a man."

"No need to gild the lily," laughed Jo as she put cups on the table and filled each of them with dark, rich coffee.

"I'm not. He is all those things and many more. I wouldn't be surprised if he hasn't already gotten father back in his debt," said Bella.

"What does Rockwell do? Gambling?" asked Alex.

"That's all I know of. Father always called him a business associate," answered Bella. "But my father is a well-respected attorney. I can't imagine what business he could have with Rockwell except the gaming."

"I still don't want you to go," said Alex. "You're right these men may be here to take you back, regardless of your marriage to me."

"I know that," said Bella. "But I need to know what their intentions are and I don't believe they will tell you without me being there."

Alex got up from his chair and paced the floor to the counter and back to the table.

"I'm coming, too," said Sam.

"No, Sam," said Alex. "I don't want to bring the law into this, yet. What if we're wrong?"

"No harm will have been done," said Sam. "I often introduce myself to strangers in town.

"What if we tell them we've been married for years and have two daughters to prove it? That I'm not the woman they think I am," said Bella not listening to Sam and Alex. Then she immediately changed her mind. "No. I don't want them to know anything about the girls."

"Good, because I don't either," said Alex.

"Well, I know it's not my call, but I agree with Bella," said Jo. "She needs to know what they look like and who they are. If they are bounty hunters like you think they might be, they won't come at you when you're expecting it. The more Bella knows the better."

"All right," said Alex. "We'll meet them together. Let's go and get that over with so we can finish our chores and get back home."

"Thank you." Bella threw her arms around Alex's waist.

He brought his arms around and held her.

"You should thank Sam and Jo. If it were up to me, then you'd stay here, but they've been bounty hunters and know from which they speak."

Jo got up, got the coffee pot and refilled all their cups. "Any idea when you are supposed to meet these men?"

"No appointment was set, Alex planned on confronting them. I'd like to get it over with and get on with our business. We need to get back and take care of the ranch," said Bella. "And I want to hold the girls, even though they'll squirm, and just tell them I love them."

Alex looked over at her like he was seeing her for the first time. It was the same look he always got when she talked about her love for their daughters. Though why he was surprised by her love for them she didn't know. If he'd just look a little deeper he could see her love for him, as well. Hard as she tried not to love him, her heart was already his.

"I'm glad you love the girls," said Alex with a smile. "They surely do love you."

She looked at him hard, willing him to understand her.

"Love is usually a two-way street."

Alex gazed at her with something akin to hunger, then his face softened, for just a moment and she knew. He loved her. Alex didn't want to, as told by the hard lines of his face now, but he did.

Bella rejoiced. As long as he loved her, she could withstand almost anything.

*****

Bella and Alex walked to the hotel from Sam and Jo's home. The journey wasn't far, only half a dozen blocks, but it took them forever as far as Bella's nerves were concerned. Normally, she would have enjoyed the walk in the beautiful July sunshine, but not today. Today, all she could think about was the two men who waited for them at the end of the stroll.

She and Alex walked into the hotel and went directly to the registration desk.

"Hello, George. Would you mind finding Miss Effie, please?" said Alex to the young man behind the desk.

"Sure thing, Mr. Hastings, be right back."

They watched him leave, headed toward the restaurant.

Effie returned a few minutes later with George following her.

"Alex. Bella. I assume you want to talk to those two men. I'll send George to their rooms and tell them you're in the restaurant. It's not too busy, but I'll put you at the first table next to the window. Thanks to Bella, I know that'll give the feeling of being in a crowd."

"Good. The more visibility the better," said Alex.

"My thoughts exactly," said the tiny woman, her blue dress matching the blue of her still-sharp gaze.

Alex led Bella to the table and held the chair for her to sit.

"Do you want coffee while you wait for them?" asked Effie. "Sure, you do. It will keep your hands busy." She signaled the waitress who brought two cups and a pot of coffee to the table.

Alex saw George reappear in the entry to the lobby followed by two men. Both were of a similar height, not much taller than George, about five feet ten inches. Alex would tower over both of them.

One man wore a gray three-piece suit with a watch in the vest pocket. His brown hair was a little on the long side, yet he sported a well-groomed mustache and beard.

The second man wore a black suit similar to the first man's but without the watch. His hair was quite short, cut above his ear and appeared to be blond. He, too, had a mustache, but no beard.

George led them to the table.

Alex stood when they arrived and until they sat. Then he sat as well.

"I'm Mr. Jones," the one in the gray suit spoke. "And this is Mr. Williams. I imagine you know why we are here."

"Even if we did, I want to hear the reason from you," said Alex.

Mr. Jones nodded. "As you wish. We have been hired by Mr. Sydney Rockwell to retrieve his fiancée, a Miss Isabella Latham. Mr. Rockwell refers to her as his stolen bride."

Bella stiffened her back and shook her head. Then she pointed at Mr. Jones. "An announcement at a party doesn't count unless I agreed. I don't. I was never his fiancée, much less his bride, regardless of what he and my father thought."

"The reasons for his referral are of no interest. We only are interested in fulfilling our contract," said Mr. Williams.

Alex rested his elbows on the table,

leaned forward, and made eye contact with each man. "Bella is married legally to me. Mr. Rockwell has no further say in any matter concerning my wife."

"We appear to be too late to prevent the marriage and, therefore, will have to leave without her. Is there any message you wish for me to give to Mr. Rockwell?" said Mr. Jones.

"You can tell the vile, toad-sucking—," said Bella.

Alex placed his hand on Bella's knee and squeezed lightly.

He narrowed his eyes, not believing for a moment they meant what they said. "My wife means to say Mr. Rockwell should stop these efforts to return her to New York. He has no legal right to do so. If you or he persists, the sheriff of Hope's Crossing will have to become involved, and none of us want that."

Mr. Jones tilted his head. "No. We certainly wouldn't want that."

"If you will excuse us, we have work to do. I would suggest you gentlemen be on the afternoon stage," said Alex.

"Thank you for your suggestion. We may take you up on it as it would appear we have no further business in Hope's Crossing," said Mr. Jones with a nod.

"Goodbye, gentlemen." Alex stood as did Misters Jones and Williams. Alex then helped Bella to her feet and clasped her by the hand as they walked out of the restaurant.

Alex looked back at the men and saw them leaning in to each other in quiet discussion. This was not over. Not by any means.

CHAPTER 11

Bella and Alex walked down the street to Smith's Mercantile. "Do you really believe they will just go away?"

Alex shook his head. "No. I don't. I want you to keep that gun with you at all times, even when you're with me."

"All right. What else can we do?"

"Nothing we haven't already done. For now, we'll keep to our regular routine."

The bell above the door to the mercantile announced them as they entered.

"Be right with you." A feminine voice came from the area of the counter in the back of the store.

"It's just us, Lavernia," said Bella.

"Bella. Alex. What are you two doing here on a Friday?" asked Lavernia.

"We'll be otherwise occupied tomorrow, so came to do our business today."

Lavernia stood behind the counter with her cash box in front of her. When she was done, she put the box under the counter.

"You want your regular order? I'll need about an hour to put it all together."

"Yes, please." Bella ran her hand over the pretty bolts of material, wishing she'd learned to sew. "I'll also need a pound of salt, an ounce of cinnamon, one jar of sorghum, an extra ten pounds of sugar and twenty-five extra pounds of flour."

"Got it. You headed to the feed store now?"

"Yes," said Alex. "Still have to get grain for the animals."

She walked around the counter.

"Effie told me about the men that come to town to see you. They've been in here and look dangerous. You two keep your wits about you."

"We will," said Bella. "Thanks for telling us."

Alex went to get the wagon from the Longworth house.

Bella watched out the window of the mercantile. She saw Misters Jones and

Williams headed her way and jumped back so she wouldn't be seen but didn't stop watching them. They passed without a glance. From the direction they were headed, she was sure they were on their way to the blacksmith, where they could rent horses.

A sick feeling that they would follow her and Alex home settled over her. Once they knew where she and Alex lived, they would also know about the girls. She'd have to keep them inside to avoid having them snatched.

When Alex returned she told him what she'd seen and what she feared.

"We must keep the girls inside until we are sure those men are gone," said Bella.

"Agreed. I'd already decided to do that."

"Poor Maddie. Maybe now would be a good time to let them have their kittens. They've been really good with Maddie when they play with him now. They only dress him up occasionally."

They started loading the wagon. Each time they went inside for another load, they discussed another point about the men and what to do.

"That's not a bad idea. I'm sure those

men will follow us home, and there is no way to lose them with the wagon."

"I thought about that. But we'll take the buggy tomorrow or perhaps we can ride."

Alex shook his head. "No riding. We'll take the buggy."

"I'm really quite a good rider. Even better than you I bet."

They finished loading the wagon and stood at the back.

"There is no way you ride better than I do. I grew up out here on my parents ranch. I've been riding since I was a child." Lord, how she missed riding. She wondered if anyone rode Champion now or if he was just left in his stall. Surely, her father would take care of her horse, if for no other reason than the animal was worth money.

"So have I. We could find out in a race."

"A race?"

"Jesse has those grays that are twins. You can't get any better match than that. Then it's just a matter of skill."

Alex furrowed his brows and bit the corner of his lip, so at least he pondered this idea before dismissing it out of hand. That gave Bella hope. Maybe he'd give in and let her ride the black if she beat him in a race.

"After all this is over, I'll race you and win. Then you'll stop pestering me about riding."

She nodded. "And if I win, you'll let me ride the black."

"Not the black."

"Yes, the black. He's the only horse you have besides Stargazer that has any spirit whatsoever and he's overflowing with it. He reminds me of my horse back in New York. Champion was full of spirit."

"That spirit is what killed Kate. That's why I only breed him now."

Bella released a pent-up breath. "When will you believe I'm not Kate and start treating me like I'm me? Stop treating me like a child."

"Then stop acting like one."

"I'm not the child here."

Bella rolled her eyes and shook her head. There was no reasoning with him when he got like this.

"We'll discuss this again at a later date, after I prove you can trust me."

"I do trust you. I let you care for my children, don't I?"

"You don't have any choice, and you know the girls love me and I love them."

Alex helped her up onto the wagon seat, and then went around the back and climbed in next to her. He took up the reins, slapped them on the horses' butts and they started walking.

The wagon was loaded down with five hundred pounds of grain in addition to all the groceries. The horses were moving as fast as they could go. They couldn't out-run a rider if they wanted to.

Bella moved her hand into her pocket, touching her gun.

Alex kept looking over his shoulder.

"You're afraid we're being followed, aren't you?"

"It's what I'd do if I was them, but if they are, they're keeping well back. I haven't seen anyone."

"We'll have to reiterate with the men the importance of keeping vigilant for any strangers."

"They know. The only one who doesn't have a gun on all the time is Jack B. When he is breaking a horse, he doesn't wear his pistols."

Bella's heart pounded and her stomach tied itself in knots. "I wish we were home."

"So do I. We're still about a mile out."

Alex looked over his should again.

This time Bella looked too and they were rewarded for their vigilance. Two riders appeared a long way behind the wagon, just cresting a small hill.

"You were right. They are following."

Alex nodded and kept his gaze ahead. "I saw."

Bella let out a deep breath. "There is nothing we can do about it. Ours is the only place out here. They were bound to find us even if they hadn't followed us."

"When we reach home, I want you to go in and corral the girls before they try to run out to greet us. I don't want those men to see them. I'll unload the wagon by myself."

Alex pulled the wagon into the side yard, next to the kitchen door. As he thought, Vi and Rose were on their way out the door when Bella stopped them.

"Who wants a stick of candy?" Bella held the bag high as she walked back into the kitchen.

The girls jumped trying to reach the bag of sweets.

When Bella reached the middle of the kitchen, she lowered the bag and each child chose her favorite flavor. Then they were headed back out the door.

"Stop," said Bella as she closed the door and stood in front of it. "Do not go outside. Your father and I want you to stay here and play with Maddie. Where is she? Have you already been playing with her? Is she hiding from you?" She put her hands on her hips and looked down at her daughters.

"Yes, Mama," said Vi. She looked at the ground and put her hands behind her back, swinging her body back and forth.

Rose stood behind Vi as was her normal stance when the girls were in trouble.

"What did you do? Did you dress her up again?"

"Yes, Mama," repeated Vi.

Bella put her hands on her hips. "If I hadn't already given you the candy, you wouldn't be getting any. So for punishment, you'll get no dessert tonight after supper and you'll get no candy stick tomorrow. Now go to your room and stay there."

Both little girls were sniffling, but no dramatic tear-filled scenes occurred.. They turned and marched up the stairs to their room.

"You're getting very good at this mothering job."

Bella whipped around and saw Alex standing in the doorway with a fifty pound sack of flour over his shoulder.

"The discipline part of it is the part I don't like." She went to the pantry and opened the flour bin for him.

He followed her in, put the bag on the floor, sliced open the top with his knife and poured the contents into the bin. "None of us do."

Bella watched him put the empty flour sack on the bin. Then he closed the pantry door, took her by the waist and brought her close. He lowered his head and sealed his lips to hers.

"Thank you for taking care of the girls."

"Always," she whispered.

Poppy pounded on the door.

"You two better get out here. There's strange fellas ridin' into the yard."

Alex opened the pantry and went to the front door.

Bella stayed in the kitchen and was glad she did. Mr. Williams came through the kitchen door.

She put herself between Mr. Williams and Poppy, and then pulled the gun from her pocket. Her pulse raced but she knew her duty. "Stop right there. Come any closer and I'll shoot."

Mr. Williams smiled. "You won't shoot me. You're only making this harder on yourself Miss Latham." He stepped forward.

Bella fired.

He went down, clutching his side.

"My name is *Mrs. Hastings*. I will never marry Sydney Rockwell."

"You shot me."

"I meant to kill you, but I can't do it while you're wounded. I'm not a murderer."

He got off the floor and pulled his hand away from his side and looked at it. The hand was covered with blood. "Mr. Rockwell is a very determined man. If it's not us someone else will come, but you will go back to New York and to Mr. Rockwell."

"Never." Fear gripped her. She knew he was right, her life would never be her own as long as Rockwell lived. "Now I suggest you get out, while the getting is good."

"I'm leaving…for now."

He disappeared through the door.

Bella shut it behind him. *We need locks on the doors and windows.*

A few minutes later, Alex appeared in the kitchen.

I heard gun fire."

Bella ran to him. "I shot Mr. Williams in the side. I was aiming for his heart."

He wrapped her in his arms. "The bastard got in. I'm increasing the watch on the house."

"What about the regular work for the men?"

"They'll do the minimum to keep the animals in good shape, but the animals are second to the safety of my family."

She leaned back in his arms and gazed up at him. "They won't stop. Sydney Rockwell won't stop until he has me. What will we do?"

He pressed her head against his chest and held her close. "We can't stop living our lives or start living them in fear. We'll take precautions and keep vigilant."

She hoped that would be enough.

*****

Saturday she and Alex went about their early chores. They had talked about canceling their plans and not going to the party, but Alex felt it was the best way to draw Misters Jones and Williams away from the house.

He was sure they were watching, so

Alex had the men pulling guard duty around the house. He told the girls they were not to go outside, but stay inside and play and he told Poppy the same thing. He was determined to make sure his girls were safe. He arranged for Poppy and Jack B to be in the house with the girls all night and tomorrow until Alex and Bella arrived home.

All day Bella's stomach roiled. She couldn't keep any food down. She told Alex her illness was due to the baby and morning sickness, but she thought it really was nerves. Every time she thought about going to the party, her stomach turned over. But she would not give in. She would not let these men ruin her life. She would not stay in hiding.

She dressed carefully for the party in the purple dress. The sweetheart neckline, open to just above her décolletage, showed the perfect amount of skin to showcase her spectacular amethyst necklace and ear bobs. This would be the last time she'd get to wear the dress for a while. Barely able to button it over her expanding stomach as it was, she'd have to talk to Alex about getting a couple of new dresses to wear while she was increasing.

When she was done dressing, Bella went downstairs to show Alex. She walked into the kitchen and saw Alex looking pretty spectacular himself.

Alex turned as she entered. Dressed in a black jacket, with white shirt that enhanced the tan of his skin, and a silver bolo tie at his neck. He had on his black wool pants and dress boots.

"You look beautiful." He walked forward and kissed her cheek.

"It's not too much? I can take off the necklace if you want."

"I didn't realize you'd brought any jewelry with you."

"I brought very little. This amethyst set and an emerald set to go with my green dress. That's all. Everything else I left at home."

"Did Sydney Rockwell buy any of that?" He waved his arm up and down in front of her.

Her eyes widened and her hand flew to her necklace. "Good gracious, no. I never took anything from him. Knowing how I feel about him, how could you even ask?"

Alex let out a deep breath and took her

hands in his. "Forgive me. That was very inconsiderate."

"It's all right. I think I'm just a little touchy lately. Normally, I wouldn't let something like that bother me."

"If you're like Kate, lots of things will bother you. She cried all the time when she was expecting."

She snatched her hands from his. "Then I'll have to make sure I don't cry at all. I'm nothing like Kate. I keep telling you that."

"Nothing wrong with being compared to her. She was a good woman."

Bella sighed. "You're right. I'm sorry. Can we just go to the party? I've got a bag packed for us to leave at the hotel. I'm assuming we'll check in before we go to Jesse and Clare's?"

"We will."

"Then I guess I'm ready. Let's go kiss the girls."

On their way to the parlor where Rose and Vi were having a tea party with their dolls, Alex dropped the valise by the front door.

"You look pretty, Mama. Can't we come with you to Uncle Jesse and Aunty Clare's house?"

"Not this time sweet things, but I promise next time we go to visit them, you both will come along. Okay?"

"Okay."

They both hung their heads looking so forlorn, Bella wished there was no danger and she could change her mind and take them along.

"Come on now. Give Mama and Daddy a hug and a kiss."

Both girls got up from the table and came to their parents. Bella dropped to her knees, regardless of her dress and got hugs and kisses from her babies.

Alex did the same.

Bella stood and brushed off her dress then turned to Poppy. "Thank you, for being here. I truly do appreciate knowing they'll be safe while we're gone."

"Of course. Anytime. It'll do you young people good to get away and be with folks your own age for a bit."

"It will," agreed Alex. "Let's go now, Bella, while we can still get there in the daylight."

"All right, I'm ready."

*****

Seventy minutes later Alex pulled to a

stop on the side of the hotel. He set the brake and then went around and helped Bella down after which he grabbed the valise from the back. Together they walked into the lobby and to the front desk.

"Hello, Mr. and Mrs. Hastings," said George from behind the desk. "We have your room ready for you, just as you requested. Here is your key, Room 107, on this floor in the back where it's quiet and it's the only guest room with a private bath," said George, as he handed over the large brass key.

"Come, my dear."

They walked down the hall to the right to the last room at the very end. Alex set the bag on the carpet and slipped the key in the lock.

Inside, Bella saw a lovely room. On the bureau was a vase with wild flowers and a bottle of wine. Through the door across from the end of the bed was a private bathroom. This had to be the nicest room in the hotel if it was the only one with a private bath. A pump was attached to the large tub, a small barrel stove with wood next to it and a metal bucket to heat the water in, was on the floor next to the stove.

"Oh Alex. It's wonderful."

She turned to him, put one arm around his neck and crooked the index finger of her other hand to bring his head down to hers.

"Thank you, husband."

She met his lips and with her tongue pressed forward. He opened and she wrapped her other hand around his neck and hung on for the ride. When they finally parted, Bella continued to hang on to him.

"You make me weak in the knees. Literally. I don't know what it is about your kisses."

"It's because you love me."

She rolled her eyes. "Don't be silly. I don't love you. You refuse to love me, so I do you as well. I'm saving my love for our children."

Alex smiled like the cat that got the cream. His finger traced gently down her cheek. "You can't resist me. Besides that, you already love me."

"I don't and I won't. Now, what time is the party? Should we go over now?"

"It doesn't start for another hour."

"What are we supposed to do until then?

He cocked an eyebrow. "I'm sure we can find something to keep us busy.

Alex tightened his hold on her and brought her close, and then he bent his head to kiss her.

Bella put her hands on his chest and pushed.

"We are not having relations. I have no desire to get out of and then back into this dress again. Besides the fabric will be wrinkled even more than it is now."

Alex didn't let her go and his smile never faded.

"Wouldn't a few wrinkles be worth it for some extra lovin'?"

She would remain strong. "It's not lovin'. It's just sex, just relations and no, a few wrinkles are not worth it."

His smile faltered and he released her.

Bella stepped away.

"Perhaps we should go early and see if we can help Jesse and Clare prepare."

Alex let out a long breath.

"Yes, I guess we should. We're certainly not having the kind of afternoon I wanted."

"Nor am I, so we might as well go."

They left and Alex locked the door behind him. They walked through the lobby. George called to them from the registration desk.

"Mr. and Mrs. Hastings."

"Yes, what is it?" replied Alex as they went toward the young man.

"Effie said I should tell you the men are still here."

"They are? Thank you, George. That's good to know," replied Alex.

"Should we take the buggy instead of walking?" asked Bella.

"I think so. At least, if we see them, we have a fighting chance of out-running them with the buggy. I've seen those horses Paul, Sam's father the blacksmith, keeps for renting. They are nothing but old nags. He said he is not loaning out prime horseflesh to folks that have probably never ridden before."

Leaving the hotel, Bella looked all around wondering if she'd see Misters Jones and Williams, but she didn't see them. Still, something felt off. She knew they were being watched.

CHAPTER 12

Alex and Bella arrived at the Donovans' about thirty minutes before the party was supposed to start.

Jesse answered the door with a look of surprise.

"Well, you two are a little early, but your assistance is requested as long as you are here."

"What do you want us to do? We are at your disposal," said Alex.

"Bella, the other ladies could use you in the kitchen and Alex, I need help rearranging the furniture."

"Certainly," said Bella as she headed to the kitchen.

When she arrived the room was in a

state of chaos. Clare, with her beautiful dark red hair done up in to a chignon and her green eyes flashing was dishing up food into large bowls. Nora, their housekeeper and cook, with an apron over her party dress and her gray hair under a cap, was loading meat onto platters.

"Hello, ladies. How about I start the dishes? Do you have an apron?"

"That would be wonderful," said Clare and Nora together.

Nora pulled out two aprons from a drawer and handed them to Bella.

"Here put both on and hopefully you won't get your dress wet."

Bella donned the aprons, then placed the stopper in the sink and poured in half of the hot water from the bucket on the stove. She pumped cold water into the bucket and the sink until both had hot but not uncomfortable water. Then she set the bucket into the oversized sink and started to wash the dishes. She rinsed them in the bucket and then put them on a dish towel to dry. Once she was done with the dirty ones, she got a clean dish towel and dried those she'd washed. Several minutes later, she waved a hand at the stack.

"All done," said Bella.

Nora handed her a pan that she'd just emptied of a rich beef gravy. "Not quite," she said.

She took the pan from Nora, washed it, dried it and put it away.

"I think I've seen every dish you own," said Bella. "Twice."

All three ladies laughed.

"Thank you both, I definitely couldn't have done this alone," said Clare.

"Any time," said Bella. "You'll have to help me if I ever throw a dinner party. Though I think it would have to be a weekend function. You'd all have to stay because we are too far out of town."

"Or just do a Saturday day thing. A picnic or barbecue. Klaus, the butcher, can get you the pig and Alex has the beef. It would be lots of fun. We'll help you plan," said Clare.

Bella was floored. These kind women were offering to help her. That was something her friends in New York would never have done. Help. With anything. She wondered if they'd really been her friends.

Slowly the house filled with people. Bella met many of the mine owners and their wives. So many people she thought she should have had a notebook to write down all their names.

The talk ranged from gold and cows to some of the women wanting to copy her dress, to babies and families. When Bella said she'd like to have lots of children some of the ladies laughed.

"You've already got two, how many more do you want?"

Bella raised her chin. "I wouldn't mind having three or four more."

"Spoken like a woman who has never gone through childbirth," said one of the older women.

Bella's eyes widened and she looked to Jo.

"It's not that bad, don't let them scare you," said Jo. "Once you have that sweet babe in your arms, you forget everything else. The pain is a distant memory."

Bella noticed Clare, who was also expecting, listening intently to the other women. Her color drained each time someone said something about the pain of childbirth.

"Clare," Bella took her hand and led her away from the women. "Don't worry about having the babe. Listen to Jo. She's the only one our age and she's already had a baby. You'll be fine."

"Bella, doesn't it scare you?"

"Of course, it does, but I will go through anything to have my children and I know you will to. You're not letting their talk scare you, you hear me?"

Clare smiled. First a small smile that barely creased her cheek until she smiled wide. "You're right. I love this baby and I'm not letting what they say scare me."

"Good. That's the spirit."

As the evening drew to a close, Bella was exhausted and exhilarated at the same time. She knew now she had good friends in Clare, Jo and Nora. The feeling was like being at home with her mother. She felt warm inside.

She hugged all her friends goodbye and walked arm in arm with Alex to the buggy.

"That was so much fun. I don't think I've ever enjoyed myself so much."

He put his hand on top of hers where it was curved around his arm.

"Even those parties you attended in New York? Surely, our little party doesn't compare."

"You're right it doesn't compare. This was fun. Nothing like those dry, boring affairs in New York."

He helped her into the buggy and started the horses down the driveway.

"Good. I'm glad you had fun."

"It was like I belonged. I've never felt I belonged anywhere."

A shot rang out, and Alex slumped in the seat.

Bella screamed. "Alex!"

She scrambled for her reticule to get her gun.

The horses, having no direction from the reins, started to run.

Out of nowhere, a rider pulled alongside, grabbed the lead from one of the horses and slowed them to a stop.

Mr. Jones appeared beside the buggy. He dismounted, pulled Alex from the conveyance and put him on the side of the road. Then he climbed in and slapped the reins on the horses and got them moving. They took the road to Bozeman.

Bella slapped Mr. Jones and tried to push him out of the buggy.

He put the reins in one hand and back-handed her with the other.

"If you don't want me to stop and tie you up, you won't do that again. And I'll take this," he pulled her reticule from her. "I don't want you to shoot me like you did my associate."

She wiped her lip. Unable to see it in the dark, she still knew from the throbbing her lips were bleeding. She thought about jumping out of the buggy, but was afraid she'd hurt the baby. She slowly pulled the pistol from her pocket and pointed it at Mr. Jones, determined to shoot him. He grabbed the barrel and pointed the gun toward the horses.

"You don't want to be doing that, *Mrs. Hastings*. Isn't it enough your husband is dead? Do you want to die, too?"

She thought of the girls and the baby she carried and relinquished the gun.

"Good girl."

Bella was being kidnapped and she hoped Alex was not dead. He couldn't be. Please, dear Lord, let him be alive.

*****

July 22, 1874
Rockwell Estate, New York City

Bella couldn't help but cry. Alex might

be dead and it was her fault. She wasn't surprised no one from Hope's Crossing came after her. After getting one of their own killed, they probably were glad to be rid of her.

What about the girls? Who would take care of them now? Martha? She wasn't a spring chicken. Raising the girls would be difficult, but Martha and her husband would see it done. Maybe Jo or Clare would take them in raise them with their children. Bella could only hope.

Misters Jones and Williams delivered her to Sydney Rockwell with her hands bound. Mr. Williams, kept his left side where she'd shot him away from her, so when she'd gotten the chance, she took her bound hands and swung them at Mr. Jones. He was not expecting it and had the black eye to show for it.

"I suggest," said Mr. Jones. "You keep her tied up. She's not come peacefully during any part of the journey."

"I'll take your suggestion under consideration."

Rather than keep her tied up, he simply kept his distance. He refused to let her contact her mother much less see her.

At their last meeting he said, "When you come around to my way of thinking and agree to marry me, I'll invite your mother to the wedding."

"Never."

"You'll see it my way soon enough. I promise you."

With those cryptic words he'd left her.

Bella paced back and forth from the bed to the fireplace and back again. The bedroom she was in was actually lovely. If it had been anywhere else she would have enjoyed having it. All the furniture was white, from the four poster bed with blue paisley canopy that matched the curtains, to the six-drawer bureau. A tall boy dresser, vanity and commode rounded out the furniture. The room was in the back of the house. She looked out her window into the garden below. No help was coming that way.

A knock sounded at the door.

What was this? Sydney never knocked.

"Who's there."

"It's Potter, the butler, miss. The seamstress is here," he said from the other side of the door.

"Seamstress?"

A key turned in the lock and then the door swung open.

Potter stood there with a formidable-looking woman dressed in a pretty blue dress.

"I'm Mrs. Covington and I'm here to take your measurements. I've been told that if you do not cooperate with me, Mr. Jones will come in and help you to cooperate."

Bella let out a long sigh. She knew what that meant. She'd be stripped of her dress and she wouldn't get it back.

"Very well. Potter, please wait outside."

"Yes, Miss Latham."

She'd given up trying to get him to call her Mrs. Hastings. The last time she'd corrected him he'd told her. "What you want me to call you doesn't matter. My employer says you are Miss Isabella Latham and that is how I must refer to you."

After he closed the door, Bella took off her dress so Mrs. Covington could measure her.

"Does he know you are increasing?"

"No, and I'd appreciate if you didn't tell him."

"I'm here because I owe him money. I don't like him any more than you do. He'll not be hearing it from me." Mrs. Covington smiled. The gesture transformed her face. No longer did she look formidable but rather kind.

"Come now, I'll make it so it hangs a bit looser and gives you room to spare without looking like it does. What color do you like?"

"My favorite color is lavender, but please make this dress dark blue. It's one of my least favorite colors, and I don't want to like this dress at all. After I'm rescued, I won't wear it again."

"I understand, but I have to make the gown appropriate for a wedding. I can make it light blue." She jotted in a small notebook.

"Very well. Thank you."

"You're welcome. I wish I could help you more. Let's get your measurements now."

Bella held her arms out parallel to the floor, while the seamstress measured her bosom, waist and hips. She measured her arms and the length from her waist to the floor and wrote down all the numbers in her notebook.

Bella lowered her arms, leaned close and whispered. "You could let my mother know

I'm here."

"Your mother? Julia Latham?"

"Yes. Do you know her?"

"Only from the newspaper."

"Newspaper?"

"Yes, she was being interviewed after her husband shot himself."

Bella's legs gave out, and she sank to the floor.

"Father...killed himself?"

"Yes, about a month ago. The article said he owed money."

"To Sydney Rockwell I would guess." He had no leverage against her now, not that he did before, because this is all forced anyway. Her father being dead made no difference to Rockwell.

"I can't say, but I wouldn't bet against you. Your mother has refused to wear mourning. She told the interviewer she would not mourn a man who abused her and was such a coward as to take his life, rather than face the consequences. She has to sell everything to pay off his debts."

"Oh, how awful. My poor mother." Tears welled in her eyes as she thought of her mother have to get rid of her belongings.

"You know, I'd say the same thing, but

the times I've seen her, she's seemed quite happy. Then I read in the society pages she's engaged to Peter Farnsworth. *The* Peter Farnsworth. The man is richer than Midas."

She slumped back in her chair. Suddenly Mr. Farnsworth helping her escape made more sense. He was in love with her mother and apparently, her mother was in love with him.

Bella laughed.

"What are you laughing at, Miss?"

"My father. He finally killed himself, because he was too much of a coward to face his debts himself and, in the process, freed my mother to follow her heart."

Mrs. Covington smiled.

"It's wonderful that something good can come out of such a tragedy."

Bella shook her head. "If you knew the man my father was, you might not say it was a tragedy."

"Why would you say that?"

Her tone harsh, her eyes narrowed. "Because my father sold me to settle his debts just a few months ago and then he gets himself into the same mess and having no more daughters to sell, he kills himself instead."

Mrs. Covington shook her head and frowned. "I'm so sorry you are in this situation. I can't imagine a father selling his own daughter. You can get dressed now, my dear. I wish I could help you. Perhaps I can try to get a message to your mother."

"Yes, please. Probably nothing she can do, but I want her to know I'm here. Perhaps Peter can help me."

"I'll do my best."

"Thank you, Mrs. Covington. I appreciate your help."

"If I could do more I would."

"Making me a comfortable gown is enough."

She picked up the purple dress. "The least he could do is have a maid come and press my dress."

"Here let me let out the seams on your dress. If it was made properly, it should have double seams so I can just clip the first seam and give you some breathing room."

The seamstress took the purple dress and with a few snips of her scissors added a full two inches to the waist of Bella's gown.

"There that should help. Let's get you dressed now before someone decides to come and report us to Mr. Rockwell."

No sooner had Bella finished buttoning her dress than the door flew open and the girth of Sydney Rockwell came through.

"What is taking so long in here? How long does getting some measurements take?"

"We're done Mr. Rockwell. I should have the dress for you in a couple of weeks."

"You have one week."

"But sir—"

He narrowed his gaze. "One week. No more."

Mrs. Covington nodded once. "Yes, sir. I'll have it done."

"And I want it pink. I like pink on my future bride, it becomes her."

"Yes, Mr. Rockwell. Pink, it is."

Mrs. Covington looked at Bella apology in her gaze.

"That's all. Get out."

Mrs. Covington winked at Bella and then hurried from the room.

"Now, my dear Isabella, you've had enough time to mourn your former husband. You'll join me for dinner tonight. I have a gift for you."

"You can keep your gifts. I want nothing from you."

He took her hand and pulled her to him.

Bella took her other hand, fisted it and hit him as hard as she could in the face.

He released her and wiped the blood from his mouth.

She'd been aiming for his eye, and hit it, but her hand slid and hurt his lip, too. Bella was glad. She rejoiced seeing him bleed.

"Don't touch me. Don't you ever touch me."

Bella turned away and walked to the window where she looked down into the garden.

"Regardless of this, you will join me for dinner. I'll see you in two hours. Potter will come for you."

She didn't acknowledge him but continued to stare into the garden until she was sure he was gone. Then she went to the bed, lay down and cried.

*****

At precisely six o'clock, Potter arrived to take her to dinner.

With dread unsettling her stomach, she followed him to the dining room where Sydney awaited her.

He sat at the end of the table, another place setting to his right, with a wrapped parcel in front of it.

He waved his arm toward the chair to his right.

"Come, my dear. Sit."

Bella allowed Potter to hold out her chair.

She smiled when she looked at Sydney. His eye was purple and his lip was split.

"I know you must be excited. You may open your gift. I'm hopeful it will make you a little bit happy."

She opened the box and inside was a nightgown of the finest silk. It was not transparent, but rather modest in its cut.

"It's beautiful."

She shuddered to think he'd want to see her in it and she was on her guard as to what he wanted in exchange.

"I want you to sleep comfortably before our wedding in eight days."

She gasped. "Eight days?"

"Yes. I've decided that will give you long enough to get used to the idea that this marriage will take place. You might as well resign yourself to it."

A single tear rolled down her cheek and if she'd been better able to control herself, even that tear would not have fallen.

"That's right, my dear. One more week and then you will be my wife. No longer will I have to refer to you as my *stolen* bride."

"Who would you speak to that you would need to refer to me at all?"

"Why anyone who was at your father's party. Most of whom are my customers, too. I'm always amazed at how many of the *upper class* are gamblers and bad ones at that."

"May I leave? I really don't have much of an appetite."

Sydney looked at her for a moment.

She was sure he would deny her.

But he nodded.

"Yes, you may go back to your room. If you get hungry, ring the bell for Potter and he will bring you a sandwich and some milk. Won't you, Potter."

"Yes, sir. At any time, day or night."

"There see? Potter will take care of you."

Bella nodded and left the table. Her heart ached. She missed Alex. Even if he'd never love her, she would have him back alive and well.

CHAPTER 13

July 4, 1874
Hopes Crossing, Montana Territory

Sam and Jo were walking home from the party. He carried a kerosene lantern so they wouldn't step in any ruts. As they walked Sam noticed what looked like someone sitting on the side of Jesse's driveway.

He walked over to the person.

"Mister." He moved the lantern closer. "This is private property—Alex?"

"Oh, my God. Is he all right? Where's Bella?"

"He's been shot in the chest. We need to try to stop the bleeding."

Sam took off his jacket and shirt, then handed the shirt to Jo.

"Press hard on the wound. It appears that man in New York has had Bella kidnapped. Stay here with Alex, I'll get the wagon so we can take him to Doc Kilarney."

Jo took the shirt from Sam and applied pressure to Alex's wound.

"Hurry. Take the lantern. You can go faster. I'm fine here with Alex."

Sam returned in what had seemed like hours to Jo. She kept turning the shirt to a different part as each got soaked with blood, but kept applying pressure to the wound in his chest. She knew Alex was losing more blood from the wound in his chest despite the pressure and the sooner Sam got there the better.

Sam pulled to a stop and jumped down. Together, he and Jo got Alex into the wagon. Sam turned the horses and galloped to Dr. Kilarney's office on the west end of town, while Jo sat in the back with Alex.

Jo climbed down without waiting for help from Sam and ran to the door. The doctor had to leave the party early due to a sick child, and Jo didn't know if he was back or not. She pounded on the door.

"Doc. Doc Kilarney."

"I'm coming," shouted the doctor.

He opened the door.

Jo blurted out. "Alex Hastings, Doc. He's been shot."

Doc hurried out to the wagon and helped Sam get Alex out of the back and into the office. They put him on a table in one of the rooms.

"We found him on the side of the road. Looks like a kidnapping. Bella is gone and so is their buggy."

"Why don't you two wait out in the other room?"

"You might need us, Doc," said Sam.

"Alex is out. Nothing I do will hurt him. Go on into the other room. If I need you I'll call."

"All right." said Sam.

"Do you have any coffee, Doc?" asked Jo.

"None made. You could go into the kitchen and make some. There are cookies in there, too, I think."

Jo was glad for something to do.

"Sure thing. Sam, come with me."

They went through the office to the back door, which led into the house. The Doc had obviously been in the office when they came or he wouldn't have heard them.

In the kitchen, Jo found the coffee beans and grinder on the kitchen counter. She took a handful of the beans and put them in the grinder then emptied the drawer with the ground coffee into the coffee pot.

After the coffee was boiled she poured herself and Sam each a cup of the steaming hot brew and took them to the table.

"Should we go back into the waiting room?" asked Jo.

"No. He'll find us here, just as easily,"

They waited. Drank the entire pot of coffee, and Jo made another, without hearing anything.

Finally, the doctor entered, looking worn out.

"Any of that coffee left?" he asked and then rolled his neck in circles.

"Sure is, Doc. You sit, and I'll get you a cup."

Jo turned back to the cupboards and got a cup for the doctor. There were cookies on the table and Dr. Kilarney sat down and grabbed one.

Sam and Jo were anxious but let the doctor catch his breath. He'd just spent three hours operating on Alex.

Finally he cleared his throat.

"Alex is lucky you found him when you did or he'd have bled to death. The bullet landed in his left shoulder and hit an artery. If I'd been able to stop the bleeding without removing the bullet, I might have left it. As it is he's going to be laid up for a few days here and then I'll send him home. What about Bella? What are you doing to find her?"

"Nothing. We know where she's headed. As soon as he knows he'll want to go after her. He can't until he is well enough to travel. We're pretty sure she's been taken to New York, back to the man her father sold her to."

"Knowing this we'll have a hell of a time keeping Alex in bed, but he needs to stay there for at least a week. That's a serious injury he's got. I'll keep him on the laudanum so he won't wake up. I think that is likely to be the only way he'll stay."

Sam and Jo left.

Doc went in to see Alex. "What have you gotten yourself into?" Doc asked his silent patient.

*****

Alex awoke and moved. The change caused him pain and he groaned.

"Bella."

Doc Kilarney went to the bed and gave him water to drink.

"You've been wounded, Alex. This is Dr. Kilarney. Can you hear me?"

"Bella."

"Bella isn't here."

"Where?"

He tried to rise.

The doctor placed his hands on Alex's shoulders.

"You've got to stay down, son."

"Don't call me, son. You're only a few years older than I am."

"Fine. You've got to stay down, Alex. You've been shot and need to heal."

He looked around taking in his surroundings and not recognizing any of it. "How long have I been out?"

"For four days. I didn't dare keep you comatose any longer. But that doesn't mean you can go chasing after your wife."

"Bella. Where is she?"

"We don't know. Whoever took her shot you and left you for dead on the side of the road. We assume it was the men who were sent here by that man in New York."

"Damn, they've got a four-day head start

on me. They are half way to Cheyenne on the stagecoach by now."

Alex tried to sit.

Doc gently pushed him back down.

"They are getting a longer head start than that. You can't go after her. Not yet. Your wound is still open."

"I don't care."

"Well you'll care soon enough when you drop dead and are no help whatsoever to Bella. Then she'll be stuck with that man forever."

Alex cursed.

"Give me two more days in bed. Then I'll see how your wound is healing. If I see good progress I'll let you go. I want you to take Sam with you."

"Sam doesn't want to go to New York."

"Why don't you ask me?" Sam pushed away from the wall behind Alex's bed.

"How long have you been back there?"

"Since early this morning," said Sam. "I've been waiting to see if the doctor would let you wake up or keep you out for another day."

"I don't want him to get hooked on the laudanum," said Doc.

Sam sat in the chair next to Alex's bed.

"They would have taken the stage which puts them seven or eight days from Cheyenne. After that they're on the train."

"What about my girls? Who has them?" Alex levered his weight onto his elbows, but pain stabbed his shoulder. Finally the doctor assisted him and placed pillows behind his back to help elevate him.

"We sent word to Poppy. She'll make sure they're all right until you get back," said Sam.

Alex relaxed back against the pillows and let out a long sigh. He was weak, weaker than he thought if just the act of sitting up made him tired. He couldn't go after Bella this way. "All right, if I stay in bed for another day, what then? We take the stage to Cheyenne?"

A bell sounded from the front room.

"I have patients to take care of. You know my feelings on this matter. You need at least two more days here in bed. After that, you can go after Bella with my blessing." Doc left the room.

"No," said Sam, answering Alex's earlier question. "We ride to Cheyenne. We can make much better time than on the stage. We could possibly save two days.

Once we get on the train, we're at the mercy of the railroad."

"Ride your fastest horse, Sam. I'll be taking the black. He's the fastest animal I have."

Sam frowned. "You haven't ridden him in more than a year. Are you sure this should be his first time out?"

"I don't have any choice." His gut churned and bile burned his throat. "I'm not letting that man take Bella away."

"You sound like a man that has fallen in love with his wife."

"I guess it took this happening for me to see it. I don't want to live without her. She's expecting you know."

Sam lifted his brows and his eyes widened. "No. I didn't. Another reason for you to take it easy, like the Doc wants. You have two people depending on you."

Alex closed his eyes and slammed his fist into the bed beside him.

"This is so frustrating. How can this happen?"

"What part of 'this' do you mean? Losing your wife, having a baby, getting shot?"

"All of it."

"Well, I can help with how the having a baby part of it came to be, but I think you can figure that one out yourself."

Sam grinned.

"Very funny."

"You expected those men to come at you on your way to the ranch, not on your way home from the party and you didn't expect them to shoot you without warning."

"You're right. I simply wasn't prepared for the kind of attack they launched against me. I should have waited and walked home with you and Jo. There are so many things I should have done."

Alex picked up the glass of water on the bedside table.

"Do you suppose the doctor has put laudanum in this water?"

"I wouldn't put it past him. He's determined you get rest, which *is* the best thing for you. But he didn't want to give you any more so the water is probably fine."

Alex took a drink.

"I want you as strong as you can be when you meet the bastard that kidnapped Bella. I figure he'll have men around him to protect him. I don't think you can just walk in and walk back out with Bella."

Alex looked away from Sam. "Assuming that she wants to go with me."

"Why wouldn't she want to come with you?"

"I told her I'd never love her and that I still love Kate."

Sam shook his head. "And do you?"

"Of course, I do." As hard as it was to share his feelings, he needed to confide in someone and Sam was his best friend. "I'll always love Kate, but not in the way Bella thinks I do. I love Bella, in some ways more than I ever did Kate. Bella is so vibrant and alive. She is so determined to make me love her and she loves my girls. How could I not love her in return?"

"But you told her that would never happen."

Alex nodded.

"What made you change your mind?"

"The kidnapping and realizing I might never see her sweet smile or see her hug the girls, ever again. I love every laugh, every tear. I just love her."

"Well, I suggest you do your best to heal. Because in two days time, I'm bringing our horses here and we're riding like the devil was after us. When we get to New

York, you'll have to look up her parents to find out where this other man is."

"Her mother will help. She has no love for Rockwell or for the father after he sold Bella to pay his debts.

"Good. I've got to see to business. I'll see you later tonight."

"I'm sleeping today as much as possible. I think Doc has laudanum in my water, because I'm feeling so sleepy now."

"See you soon."

*****

Sam sent word to the Hastings ranch that Alex wanted the black stallion brought into town along with a satchel of clothing and that he was going after Bella. He wouldn't be back for a month and would Poppy bring the girls into town to Jo Longworth?

The next day a wagon driven by Jack B, carrying the girls with the black horse tied to the back, came into town from the Hastings ranch. Jack B dropped the girls off at Sam and Jo's house and took the big black horse to the barn behind it. An empty stall became home to the spirited black stallion. Jack B put oats, hay and water in the stall with the horse.

At Alex's request, Sam took Violet and

Rose to see their father.

"Daddy, what you doing here at the doctor's house?" asked Vi. Always the bolder of the two, she was often the one to speak for them both.

Alex reached out his hand and stroked her hair. "Well, sweetie, some bad men shot your daddy and took Mama away. Daddy is going after your mama to bring her back home."

"You mean Mama didn't want to leave us?" Vi's eyes were wide and filled with tears.

"No, your mama didn't want to leave you. She'll never want to leave you, she loves you."

Her tears fell. "But our first mama left. She died."

"Bella is not dead." Alex said it with more force than he meant to.

Wide-eyed, Vi and Rose both took a step back.

"I'm sorry. I didn't mean to scare you. Daddy will bring back Mama. The bad man is going to wish he was dead when your daddy gets done with him."

"Good," said Vi.

"Good," echoed Rose.

"We don't want no one to hurt our mama." Vi sat on Alex's right side, next to Rose.

He closed his arm around them and held them to him.

Both girls started squirming within the first two minutes. The little balls of energy were ready to go.

Alex released them.

They stood away from the bed but stayed close.

"Daddy, when are you gonna get Mama back? We miss her."

Alex laughed.

"Do you miss me, too?"

"Yeah, but you're here. We want Mama, too."

He sobered. His little darlings said it best. He wanted their mama, too. No one was keeping him away from his wife. Not now, not ever.

Alex looked up at Sam. "We leave at first light."

CHAPTER 14

July 23, 1874
New York City

Alex and Sam made good time. They rode for hours stopping only to let the horses rest and take a quick nap themselves. Doing so, they made it to Cheyenne in six days. The train to New York took another seven days from Cheyenne and they had to switch trains in Chicago.

Finally they reached New York. They took a cab to the Latham home. Alex was so anxious he couldn't keep his legs still in the cab.

Upon arriving, Alex dashed out of the conveyance and up the steps to the front door. Sam paid the driver and followed Alex who was pounding on the front door.

The butler answered.

"Gentlemen. May I tell my mistress who is calling?"

"Tell her Alex Hastings, her son-in-law, is here to see her."

The man lifted an eyebrow and then nodded. "If you will follow me."

The butler held the door open.

"If you'll wait here, I'll get my mistress."

Alex thought it odd the butler referred to Bella's mother as his mistress.

"Do you suppose she quit using her husband's name because of the debts? Though from the look of this house, you wouldn't think they'd be in debt."

Alex couldn't believe his eyes. Rich, thick carpeting cushioned their footsteps, marble stairs to his left led to the second and third floors. Windows were on either side of the door and above it was stained glass. To come from all this wealth, Bella must have thought him dirt poor, but she never complained, never said a word.

"No, Mr. Hastings, I quit using the name Latham, because it disgusts me. Now where is my daughter? Why isn't she with you?"

Alex whipped around at the sound of her voice.

Julia Latham was a beautiful woman. Her blonde hair had yet to gray and was in a bun off her neck. As she got closer, he saw the green dress she wore matched her eyes.

"Rockwell kidnapped her."

"I should have known. I assume you are here to get her back?"

"Yes. I want my wife back."

"Good. And who is your quiet friend?" She jutted her chin toward Sam.

Alex put his hand on Sam's shoulder. "He's my friend, Sam Longworth and the sheriff of Hope's Crossing."

"I'm Julia Latham, but I prefer to be just Julia."

She extended her hand to both men in turn. Alex could see Bella in her mother. The same eye shape and the same full lips.

"Come with me we can talk in the library, away from prying eyes."

"I'll wait in the foyer. You two need to talk alone," said Sam.

"Thank you, Sam," said Alex. He followed Julia. "I'm sorry your husband felt the need to take his life."

Julia fisted her hands. "Don't be sorry for him. He was a coward who sold *my* daughter to pay his gambling debts. May the Lord forgive him, because I *never* will."

"*Your* daughter?" said Alex. "Shouldn't it be 'our' daughter?"

"No. Ernst was not Isabella's father. She did not know but he never let me forget the fact, not that I would have wanted to. I was glad Ernst was not her father. Then, when Rockwell took an interest in her, Ernst saw a way to get his debt paid and exact retribution from me, too."

"Who is Bella's father?"

"Please be seated, Alex." She pointed at the two leather chairs in front of the massive dark wood desk. "No one you would know. His name is Peter Farnsworth."

Alex sat.

Julia remained standing and then she paced between the desk and the fireplace.

Alex could not remain seated. The churning in his stomach was too great. He needed to know where Bella was, but got the impression that he should listen to Julia first.

"Bella mentioned him. He helped her escape and she thought there might be something between you two. She said he was always kind to her, even or maybe especially, when her father was not."

Julia's face softened.

"He has always loved her. He tried to get me to leave Ernst, but I could not bring that kind of infamy down on Peter. He's a good man. He did nothing but love me, and I him. My parents contracted with Ernst for my hand in marriage. He was much older than I. Perhaps that's why he thought selling Bella was all right. Since that was how he got his wife, why not let Rockwell have the daughter he never wanted to claim?"

"Where can I find Rockwell? I must get to Bella. He's already had her for days. She must be terrified."

"Not my Bella. She'll fight to the very end. You must not discount that. She's smart and feisty. If something has happened you must not hold it against her."

Julia came forward and put her hands on Alex's chest.

"You must promise me you will not hold anything that may have happened against Bella. If you cannot promise me this then I will have her father, Peter, rescue her and bring her to his home. She will be safe there."

Alex took Julia's hands in his. "I love Bella. She carries my child. There is nothing Rockwell could do to her that will change my love for her."

Julia smiled. "Your child. That's wonderful. She will be stronger knowing that you love her."

Alex looked away.

"I was not smart enough to tell Bella of my love. She still believes I am in love with my late wife, Kate. Don't misunderstand. I still love Kate, but I never felt for her what I feel for Bella. The all consuming fire I feel for her. The gentle peace she gives me when she's near. The way she loves my daughters."

"Wait," said Julia. "You have children?"

"Yes, two four-year-old twin girls. They call Bella mama. I cannot go home without her. They cannot lose another mother."

"Yes, I can see my Bella with children. She would love them. Love is something she has a lot to give. Very well, I'm convinced you do indeed have Bella's best interests at heart."

"Where is she?"

Julia pulled the servant cord.

A butler appeared moments later.

"Walters, please have the carriage brought around."

"Yes, mistress."

"Thank you for loaning us your carriage," said Alex.

"Don't be thanking me. I'm going with you. Unless I'm greatly mistaken, Bella will need me. Sydney is not known as a patient man, but he's never been faced with someone like Bella. Let me get my coat."

Alex followed Julia out of the library and to the foyer, where Sam waited.

"Wait here just a moment. I shall return."

She turned and climbed the curved staircase.

"Return?" asked Sam.

"She's coming along."

"Why? She'll just get in the way."

"She thinks Bella will need her and I believe she may be right."

Julia returned shortly wearing a long, dark green coat and pulling on black gloves.

"Shall we go?" she asked. "The carriage should be waiting."

They walked outside where a large black coach awaited.

The butler, Walters, held the door open

and assisted Julia into the conveyance ahead of Alex and Sam.

When they were all seated, Julia took a stick and used it to pound on the ceiling. The carriage set off with a lurch, after which the ride was smooth.

"The distance is not great. You should prepare whatever it is you are planning to get inside the house."

"I plan on knocking on the door," said Alex. "And, if I have to, I'll break down the door."

Julia lifted an eyebrow. "I do believe you will."

Alex looked out the window and saw the coach turn up a long drive.

"Prepare yourselves, gentlemen. We are about to arrive."

*****

July 22, 1874

Bella excused herself as soon as he would allow. She took the box and raced up the stairs. Anxious to get out of the dress and wash herself she closed the door and wished someone would come behind her to lock it.

No sooner had she wished it than she

heard the lock click in place. Potter must have followed her.

Bella dropped the box on the floor and kicked it to the wall, she would not wear anything Sydney gave her.

She unbuttoned her dress and dropped it at her feet. It was followed by her corset, chemise and bloomers. Bella stepped out of the clothing and walked to the commode and washed herself with the soap and water found there. Then she put back on her chemise and bloomers.

Bella allowed her vigilance to waver and walked to the looking glass. It was cheval glass and quite expensive she knew.

She turned sideways and looked to see if her baby showed yet. There was a small bump, but mostly she was just getting thicker up and down her entire middle, not just her stomach.

She put back on her corset and dress. Exhaustion felled her and she went to the bed, turned down the blankets and crawled beneath just the sheets. She was asleep almost before her head hit the pillow.

Bella didn't know what it was that awoke her. She sensed a presence, a sinister presence. Sydney was in the room.

To keep from screaming she covered her mouth with her fist.

Moonlight coming through the window illuminated Sydney's bulk as he stood at the end of her bed, watching her. He was in his dressing gown and didn't come nearer, thank God.

"I know you're awake. I'm not bedding you tonight. But after we're married, you will be mine."

After uttering those words he turned and left through the door that connected his bedroom with this one.

Bella shook with both fear and rage. She would die before she let Sydney Rockwell take her.

The next morning was July 23rd. Nineteen days since she'd been taken. Nineteen days since her beloved Alex had been shot to death. It was her fault. *All her fault.* If she'd never run to begin with, she would never have met Alex and their beautiful daughters would still have a father.

A knock sounded on the door.

"It's Potter, miss. Time for breakfast."

A key turned in the lock and the tall, gray-haired man entered.

"I'm not hungry, Potter."

"I don't blame you, miss. But I have my orders and I cannot leave this room without you."

Bella saw the earnestness in his face and knew he would wait there, gathering the ire of his employer, rather than lose his job for not bringing her down.

"Very well. I'll come with you. I don't want you to get in trouble, Potter."

"Thank you, miss."

She walked out of the room and started down the hall.

"Miss Latham, I shouldn't tell you this, but Mr. Rockwell has ordered Judge Harrison to come to the house this afternoon and your dressmaker is to be here at ten o'clock. I believe he plans on marrying you today."

Bella closed her eyes and leaned against the wall. *Dear God what will I do now?*

She entered the dining room and found Sydney at the table. He held his coffee cup with one hand and the newspaper with the other.

"Come, my dear. Sit. Have some breakfast. You must keep up your strength."

Her eyes widened. *Did he know about the baby?* Her first response was to cover her stomach. Luckily she'd squashed that notion, immediately—she didn't want to bring attention to her baby.

She walked forward and sat at his right.

Potter brought her a plate piled high with eggs, sausages, sweetbreads, toast and a cornmeal muffin.

At the sight of the sweetbreads, Bella's stomach roiled and she struggled not to vomit. She pushed the plate away.

"Just coffee, please, Potter."

"Yes, miss."

He took the plate away and returned with a cup of coffee, a small pitcher of cream and the sugar bowl.

Bella added sugar and cream to the coffee and sipped. She closed her eyes and made sounds of pleasure.

"What I would give for you to make those sounds when you're lying with me," said Sydney.

"I'll never lie with you, regardless of what you may force me to do. My heart will always belong to my *husband*, Alex."

Potter returned to the room with Mrs. Covington in tow.

"Ah, Mrs. Covington, you are just in time. Isabella, go with her and put on your wedding dress. I won't have my bride be in the wrinkled mess that you are now. Go."

Bella rose from the table and accompanied the seamstress. They arrived in the bedroom and Potter closed the door behind them, locking it.

Bella turned to her.

"Were you able to get a message to my mother?"

"No. Mr. Rockwell had one of his servants in my shop watching so no one worked on anything but this dress. I had no way to get a message past his guard."

Bella sighed deeply and then patted the woman on the shoulder.

"It's all right. I should have known that's what he would do."

"We had best get you into this dress. I'm sorry I don't have a clean corset for you, but I did bring a new chemise and bloomers. You will at least feel fresher with clean garments against your skin."

"Thank you. That was very kind of you to do."

"It is nothing. I wish I could do more."

Bella unbuttoned the purple dress and let it fall to the floor, followed in quick succession by her chemise and bloomers.

She set the corset on the bureau, next to her.

She dressed again in the clean clothes and then put the pink dress on. The dress flowed down from a fitted waist. A small bustle with a large lace-covered bow over the top was sewn into the back of the dress so no metal cage was needed.

"I tried to make this your dress, not his. I filled the low neckline with lace that matches the cuffs and the bow. I don't want you to look at this dress and think of him, but to think of how you defied him. Do you understand?"

"Yes. Thank you. The dress is beautiful and I shall think of you and all you tried to do for me, when I wear it."

"Now, Judge Harrison accompanied me in the carriage here. I believe he was quite surprised by this turn of events. He said he had cleared his calendar for this afternoon, not this morning."

"Rockwell was in my bedroom last night, just watching me. He doesn't want to wait any longer." Bile rose in her throat at the memory.

A knock sounded on the door and then the key turned in the lock.

Potter pocketed the key as he stood

there.

"Mr. Rockwell is ready for you to join him in the library. He and Judge Harrison await you. I'm sorry, miss."

"Thank you, Potter."

"Come now, dear. Hold your head high," said Mrs. Covington.

Bella nodded, the knot of fear in her throat was so large, speech was impossible.

The three of them walked down to the library. At the door, Mrs. Covington turned to leave.

"Please, ma'am, Mr. Rockwell requests you and I act as witnesses."

With a deep sigh, she nodded.

Potter opened the door and Bella walked through first.

"Ah, there is my dear, Isabella and looking so beaut—"

He walked forward, grabbed the lace that filled the neckline and pulled, ripping the lace from the dress.

"Ow, you're hurting me," cried Bella, her hands holding her neck where the collar had pulled off when he ripped the lace.

He turned to Mrs. Covington and backhanded her.

"I did not give you leave to change the

design of the dress. I was very specific as to what I wanted. Next time you will do as I instruct you."

With a whimper, her hand on her face, Mrs. Covington nodded.

"See here, Sydney, there is no need for violence," said Judge Harrison.

"Don't you start, Harrison. I'm tired of my wishes being ignored."

The judge put up his hands in front of him and backed away.

"Now, let's get started. The short version, Harrison."

Bella stood next to Sydney. He held her hand in a crushing grip. She tried to pull her hand away and beat on his chest with her other hand.

He grabbed her by the upper arms and shook her, rattling her. Then he turned her around to face the judge but kept his arms around her so she couldn't hit him again.

"Dearly beloved," the judge intoned. "We are gathered before these witnesses to join this man and this woman in holy wedlock. Do you Sydney Philip Rockwell take this woman to be your lawful wedded wife to have and to hold, for richer or for poorer, in sickness and in health and to keep yourself only unto her from this day forward?"

"I do." Sydney's voice rang out, filling the room.

"And do you Isabella Maria Latham, take this man—"

"No. Never."

"I think we can skip her vows Harrison and just say yes for her," said Sydney quickly.

"Sydney, that is highly improper, I—" said the judge.

"Don't forget what you are getting out of this arrangement,"

The judge swallowed hard and started again.

"Do you have a ring?" asked Judge Harrison.

"I do but I don't think she'll wear it right now. I'll give it to her later," said Sydney.

"Then by the powers vested in me by the City of New York and the State of New York, I now pronounce you man and wife. You may kiss the bride."

Sydney released her and though shorter than Bella he turned her around to face him as if to kiss her.

"You try and I'll bite you," said Bella.

He quickly pulled back his head.

"I can see you will need some special things before we can consummate our marriage."

"Potter, send for Mr. Jones and Mr. Williams."

"Yes, sir."

Potter hurried off to do his employers bidding.

"Thank you, Harrison. Your debts are paid in full."

"I will make sure not to get in your debt again," said the judge. "The price to pay them is too high."

Sydney laughed.

"You'll be back. You always are," gloated Sydney

Judge Harrison left the room.

"Mrs. Covington, as for you, only half your debt is paid. You deliberately changed the design of the dress from what I wanted by putting in the lace and look at it now. It's ruined. She'll never be able to wear it again."

"I tried to make it something she *could* wear again," said Mrs. Covington, who spoke for the first time. "The design you had was appropriate only for the bedroom. She would not have been able to wear it in public without causing a scene."

"Perhaps. That's why you are getting half of your debt to me written off."

"Very well."

She looked over at Bella.

"Goodbye, my dear."

The little woman walked out.

Bella was alone with Sydney Rockwell.

"Come upstairs, Isabella."

"No."

He grabbed her wrist before she could step out of his reach. His grip was like iron and he pulled her with him out of the room and up the stairs to the master bedroom.

Once there he released her and locked the door, putting the key in his suit jacket pocket.

"You can take off your dress now. Perhaps you would even try to seduce me to let you go. It won't happen but you can try. I would enjoy it very much if you would try."

Her stomach roiled at the thought. "Never. You disgust me."

"As my wife you will learn not to be disgusted by me. I can be very nice when you are nice to me. I'll shower you with jewels, silks…whatever you want."

She backed away toward the window, staying far from the bed. "I want my freedom. I want to go back to Hope's Crossing and raise my daughters. You killed their father. I'm all they have left."

"Bring them here. I will help you raise them."

"No. Do you think I want your foul stench to touch them? They are better off being raised by strangers."

He seemed content to stand by the door. Waiting.

Misters Jones and Williams would be there soon and then what would happen.

"Why did you send for your henchmen?"

"Because I can't tie you to the bed by myself."

Bella shook her head. "No. Never." She went to the window and tried to raise it but it was locked.

A knock sounded on the door.

Sydney unlocked and opened the door. Mr. Jones stood there with Mr. Williams behind him.

"You wanted us for what reason, sir?"

"I want you to tie her to the bed."

Bella took the curtains, put them over

the window and shoved her fist through. The glass ripped the curtain and cut her hand.

"Yes, sir."

Both men advanced on Bella.

She climbed on the window seat.

"No, you don't," said Mr. Jones.

He grabbed the back of her hair and pulled her back from escape.

"No," cried Bella.

Mr. Williams grabbed her hand and together the two men pulled her to the bed.

Sydney handed them the sash to one of his robes.

Bella fought. She kicked with her feet and hit at them with her fists, but they kept out of reach. Mr. Jones got her left wrist tied to the mahogany bed post.

Mr. Williams backhanded her before he tied her right wrist to the other bed post with a silk cravat. "I owe you for shooting me."

Then they did the same with her ankles with two more cravats.

She couldn't move.

"Thank you, gentlemen. Your fee will be sent to you by courier later today."

"Yes, sir."

Misters Jones and Williams left and Sydney locked the door after them.

"I don't want any disturbances while I seal our wedding vows."

"I'm married to Alex Hastings and I'll never be married to you."

"Ah, but you're not married to him anymore. I saw to that. Your husband was killed by my men on my order. I didn't want any jealous husband to come to your rescue."

'No." The sound was a whimper as her tears flowed. She'd hoped Alex was still alive.

"Yes, my dear. Now we seal our vows."

He at least spared her the sight of him undressing, instead he went into his closet and changed into a robe before returning.

"Now, I should cut you out of that dress, I do so want to look at you, but I want you beneath me more."

He raised her skirt and tugged at her bloomers, but they would not move down her legs because he had them spread so far apart.

Bella started laughing.

"What's the matter, Sydney? Thwarted by your own hand?"

"It matters not. I have scissors for just such an occasion."

She would goad him to impotence, anything to save herself from his touch. "You have to tie up every woman, don't you? No one would have relations with you willingly. I bet you can't even buy sex can you?"

Sydney got his shears and cut away her bloomers.

"As long as I have the scissors handy, I'll cut your dress open, too. I want to see you in all your glory."

"No. Please stop," cried Bella. Fear coiled within her. She couldn't stop him and she was ashamed and sick.

He'd cut the skirt up to the waist and was starting on the bodice when the door came crashing in.

CHAPTER 15

The carriage stopped. Alex exited first and then helped Julia down.

Sam followed.

They approached the red brick mansion with four white two-story marble columns in the front.

Alex banged the great brass knocker on the door. If someone didn't answer this door, he'd break it down.

A middle-aged man answered.

"May I help you, sir?"

"I want to see your employer. Where is Sydney Rockwell?"

"I'm sorry sir, my employer is unavailable. This is his wedding day, you see."

Sam stepped through the door and into the foyer with the butler's shirtfront in his hands and lifted the man off the floor.

"If you don't tell him where Rockwell is, I'll let him make mince meat of your face," said Sam.

The butler put up his hands.

"Don't hurt me, sir. Mr. Rockwell is in the master bedroom with his new wife."

Sam shook the man.

"Where?" asked Alex.

The butler pointed upstairs.

"It's the first door on the right, sir."

Sam dropped the man and ran up the stairs behind Alex, who was taking them three at a time. Outside the door they both stopped and listened.

Alex heard Bella cry out and his anger knew no bounds. He slammed his shoulder against the door and the jamb splintered. He and Sam both shouldered the door and it crashed to the floor.

He saw Rockwell, his robe hanging open and underneath he was naked as the day he was born. He was on the bed over Bella with a pair of scissors cutting off her dress.

"Rockwell!"

Rage propelled Alex into the room like a

raging bull. Despite his wound, anger gave Alex strength enough to shove the huge, fat man from the bed throwing him to the floor.

Rockwell lay on his side, not moving.

Alex kicked him.

"Get up you coward."

Still Rockwell didn't move.

Alex turned him over.

Rockwell was dead, the scissors buried deep in his chest.

Alex felt only relief.

"Bella!"

"Alex. You're alive."

Tears streamed down her face.

He worked to untie her as quickly as he could. When she was free, he took her into his arms.

"I'm sorry, Alex. I'm so sorry. So glad you're alive. Oh, Alex." She kissed his face all over and held him close.

"Shh. We're together nothing else matters."

Sam and Julia came into the room.

When Bella saw Julia she cried out. "Mama."

Julia took her coat off, hurried forward, covered Bella and then wrapped her arms around her daughter.

"You're fine now, my darling daughter. It's all right. Everything will be just fine, you'll see."

Bella shook her head and cried.

Alex couldn't do anything but stand by and let his wife be comforted by her mother. All he wanted was to take Bella in his arms again and hold her and tell her he loved her, but he couldn't do any of that right now.

Julia looked over her shoulder.

"She needs me right now, as I was afraid she might. Let me help her work through this. You need to get the police. Have Potter, the butler, send someone for them. I'll take care of Bella."

"I'll get the police," said Sam.

Alex's chest hurt like hell, but it wasn't his wound that bothered him. *He* wanted to comfort Bella, and she wanted nothing to do with him. She probably thought all of this was his fault, that he didn't protect her as he should have, as he vowed to do when they married. That was what he felt, why shouldn't she feel the same?

He nodded to Julia and followed Sam out of the room.

"She's traumatized right now and wants her mother to soothe her," said Sam. "Don't worry, Bella will be fine, and then, so will you."

"I don't know if that's true or not. She doesn't want anything to do with me and she's probably right not to," said Alex. "I let this happen to her. I let her down."

Sam put his hand on Alex's shoulder. "You were shot and I'll bet she thought you dead, but she still fought. He had to tie her down, she fought so much."

Alex lifted his head. "She did, didn't she?"

"Yes. Give her time, Alex, time to get over what happened to her at his hands."

They watched Julia and Bella come down the stairs.

"Potter," said Alex. "Send someone for the police. Your employer has been killed."

"Good," said the butler under his breath. "Yes, sir. Where shall I say you are, should they want to talk to you?"

Alex looked over at Julia. "Where are we going?"

"To Peter Farnsworth's," said Julia. "4801 West Colonial Drive."

"I'll be there with *my wife* and her mother."

"Very good, sir."

In the carriage, Alex could not catch Bella's gaze. She kept her head buried in Julia's shoulder.

It tore up his heart to see her like this, so vulnerable.

When they got to the Farnsworth home, Alex stepped out of the carriage as the door to the house opened.

Peter Farnsworth stepped out of the house.

Alex helped Julia and then Bella down. She still didn't look at him.

"Julia. Bella. Come in. Come in. Walters sent word you'd gone after Bella. I hoped you'd come here." said Farnsworth.

"Peter," said Julia. "I brought her here because I don't want her being any place where she has bad memories. She has only good ones of this place and of you."

"I know. Follow me," said Mr. Farnsworth.

Alex could see Bella in this man. He had the same golden brown hair and brandy-brown colored eyes, though he was tall, nearly as tall as Alex. Julia on the other hand was the same height as Bella and just as curvy. His beautiful Bella was the best of both her parents.

"Peter," said Julia. "This is Alex Hastings, Bella's husband and his friend Sam Longworth. They will be staying as well."

"You're welcome gentlemen."

"Thank you for helping us, sir," said Alex. "I greatly appreciate what you are doing for Bella. She means the world to me."

Bella's step faltered, but then she leaned on her mother and they followed Peter up the grand curving staircase. They turned down the first hallway on the right. The walls were painted white, with incredible scroll work at the top of the walls and on the columns that marked the entrance to the hall. Thick, dark blue carpet silenced their footsteps, so even their breathing could be heard.

Alex thought Bella might appreciate the opulence after the simple life she now had. What if she didn't want to go back to that life? Surely she loved his daughters enough, even if she didn't love him, to return.

"Gentlemen," said Peter. "Sam, you may have the first room on the left, Alex, the second. The first room on the right is my room, Julia's is next to that and Bella's is across the hall, next to Alex's room."

Neither Sam nor Alex stopped to look in their rooms but followed Julia and Bella.

Peter opened the door to Bella's room and ushered the women inside.

Julia turned in the doorway and stopped Alex. "Let me be with her for a while, get her calmed down."

"Julia," Alex whispered. "How am I to tell her I love her if she won't see me."

She placed her hand on his arm and whispered back. "You'll be able to. If not before, then tonight after dinner. Peter has wonderful gardens. Take her for a walk. Keep it light. Let her get used to being your wife again."

"What about the baby? Could that bastard have hurt the baby?"

Julia shook her head. "No. I believe we got there before he could do anything more than terrorize her."

"If I could kill him all over again I would and it would not be by accident this time." Alex pounded his fist into his hand. He wanted to hit the wall or better yet Rockwell. The villain's accidental death brought no satisfaction. Yes, he was gone and couldn't hurt anyone else. That was a good thing, but Alex wanted to make him hurt like he had Bella. But he couldn't, so he would concentrate on Bella and help her in any way he could to get over this trauma.

"I understand your feelings," said Julia. "I have the same ones myself. The only good thing that ever happened because of Rockwell is he chased Bella to you."

Alex took his hat off and ran a hand through his hair. "I'm not sure Bella feels that way."

"But I do."

At her familiar voice, Alex's head whipped up and he stared at Bella over Julia's shoulder. She was still wearing Julia's coat

"Bella."

Julia moved back and he walked toward Bella. If she could only feel the love in his heart.

She ran to him and leapt into his waiting arms, wrapping her arms around his neck.

"Oh, Alex. I was so scared. I thought you were dead and I'd never see you or the girls again."

He wrapped his arms tightly around her wanting to never let her go. To hell with the pain in his shoulder. It was worth any pain to have Bella back in his arms.

"Bella. My Bella. I was shot, that's why I didn't come sooner. Doc wouldn't let me go until I'd healed enough to make the trip without dying on the way. It killed me to wait. And without you knowing how I feel. I was so afraid you'd give up on me."

"I prayed constantly that you survived. How *do* you feel?"

She brushed a long lock of hair back out of his eyes.

"I love you, Bella. I've never loved anyone the way I love you. My heart longs for you. I love the way you laugh. The way you love my daughters. The way you're always after me to ride the black. I love everything about you and wouldn't change you for anything."

Her eyes widened and filled with tears. One trickled down her cheek.

"I've waited so long to hear those words."

He caught it with his finger and brought it to his lips. "No more tears, love. We're together now."

Alex captured her lips with his and put all the love he felt into his kiss. He met her tongue and caressed it. He pulled back and placed his forehead against hers.

"I'm never letting you out of my sight again."

She smiled.

"Of course, you will. We have our life to lead together and with the girls."

Bella got a worried look on her face.

"What about the girls? Who has them? Are they all right?"

"They're fine. They are with Jo."

She relaxed and leaned against his chest.

"They will enjoy that. They do love playing with little Paul."

"It's good practice. They'll be ready when their baby brother or sister gets here."

A knock sounded on the open door behind them.

Alex looked around to see Julia. Apparently, she and Sam had left them alone when Bella came up to Alex. He was so happy to have Bella with him he hadn't noticed.

"I have clothes for you. I thought some of my dresses might fit you better than your old ones," said Julia. "I'm a little larger around the middle than you are."

"Thank you, Mama."

Julia smiled. "I put them in Alex's room

and I had his and Sam's valise's brought from the Latham house as well. You're married after all and you two should be together," said Julia.

"Thank you. You've been very kind," said Alex.

"Nothing kind about it. She will always be my daughter. I'm simply being her mother."

"I want to get out of this horrible dress. Now." Bella looked down at herself, still covered with Julia's coat.

Alex and Bella walked back to his room. He opened the door and ushered Bella inside, closing the door behind him.

Alex looked around them. "They must call this the green room."

"I would guess you are correct."

Everything was done in shades of green, from the rich, dark color of the carpet on the floor to the heavy brocade curtains on the window seat and the canopy on the mahogany bed. The rest of the furniture in the room matched the bed, all dark wood. The room was definitely made for a man.

"Did your mother tell you?"

"Tell me what?"

"Ernst Latham was not your father."

Bella took off the coat and placed it on the bed. Then she removed the dress and undergarments and put them in a heap in the corner.

"If he wasn't my father, who is?"

"Didn't you tell me that someone had always been kind to you and your father never was?"

Her eyes widened.

"Peter. Peter Farnsworth is my father?"

"Yes. Apparently they were in love and had planned on marrying, when your grandfather arranged for Julia to marry Ernst Latham."

"So Mother was sold as well."

"It would appear so. I should have let her tell you, but I didn't want you to grieve over a man who wasn't even related to you."

"He raised me."

"No. Your mother raised you. Ernst tolerated you because he couldn't produce children of his own, as shown from the many years of marriage with no other offspring."

Bella donned a clean chemise and bloomers, then chose a sky blue dress with lace at the collar and cuffs. It fit her quite well.

"You and I can buy you some new clothes tomorrow if you like. I'm not a pauper, you know. Or we can just stay here in bed and make love all day."

Bella stiffened.

"What's the matter, love?"

"I…I…" She let out a long breath. "I'm not ready to make love, yet. All I can picture is him over me."

"That's why we need to replace that image in your mind to one of me. I love you, Bella. I will never hurt you."

She crossed over to him and ran her fingers down his cheek.

"I know. I just need some time."

"You can have all the time you want. I'm not leaving you."

"Thank you for understanding."

"Thank your mother for that. She warned me you might need her and need time. I planned on taking you for a walk in Peter's gardens tonight. Would you like that?"

"Yes. Very much."

*****

That night after dinner they all went to the library for drinks and cigars. Julia and

Peter didn't hold to traditions where men and women separated after dinner. Instead they preferred to remain together and discuss the day's events. Julia enjoyed a brandy after dinner, while Peter and Sam imbibed Jameson Irish whiskey.

"It's the best Irish whiskey to be had anywhere," said Peter, standing in front of a beautiful oriental cabinet inlaid with mother of pearl on the doors. He poured two fingers in each of two glasses and handed one to Sam. He then poured a similar amount of brandy for Julia.

The three took seats around the fireplace, where a dark brown leather sofa was framed on either end by a matching chair. Sam took the chair and Peter and Julia the sofa. Peter put his arm around Julia's shoulders and she relaxed into him.

Alex and Bella stood at the doors to the garden. Bella kept her arm hooked around Alex's. She didn't ever want to let go of him, afraid she might lose him for real next time.

"Bella and I are taking a stroll around your gardens, Peter. I've got it on good authority they are some of the best to be seen. I saw lamps lighting the walkways from our room."

"Yes, there are plenty of lamps, so you won't get lost. But Julia is biased since she helped me to design them."

"But how? Father…I mean Ernst, never would have allowed you to come here to help with the gardens," said Bella.

Julia laughed. "Ernst made my life as miserable as possible, that's true, but once a week when he was at work, I would go shopping and meet Peter at the bookstore. There we would talk and design. Meeting with Peter is what kept me sane all those years."

"When will you two get married?" asked Bella. "I'm ready to have my real father in my life."

Peter's eyes glistened. "I'm ready to be in your life as well. Your mother and I have been discussing this and decided we're coming along when you go back to Hope's Crossing. We thought we might get married there."

He held Julia's hand in his and brought it to his lips, placing a kiss on the inside of her wrist.

"I'm not taking the chance of losing her again. And I own a very nice rail car we can take as far as possible, which should make the journey more comfortable for everyone."

Alex walked over to Peter and shook his hand.

"We'd love for you to come to Hope's Crossing and stay with us as long as you like. But I warn you our lifestyle is very simple. It's not like living here. We have a housekeeper and cook, but otherwise do for ourselves. You do however have two granddaughters who will love to meet you."

"I can't wait," said Julia. "To meet the little ones who stole my Bella's heart."

"And they have, completely. Wait until you meet them Mama. Violet is the one who does most of the talking for them both, but Rose sticks up for herself when she needs to. They are such beautiful girls." Bella gazed at Alex, smiling at her one true love. "The best of both their parents. The long dark hair of their handsome father and their mother's green eyes. You'll love them."

"I'm certain I will. I'm looking forward to being a grandmother," said Julia.

"And I a grandfather, as well as a father and, finally, after all these years, a true husband to my only love," said Peter, his gaze on Julia and his arm around her shoulders.

Her mother gazed up at Peter.

Bella saw there the love she had for him. It was a look she'd never seen her mother give Ernst. Bella smiled.

Bella couldn't think of the man who had raised her as anything but Ernst. "Peter, I know you don't know me very well, but," Bella paused, "do you think you'd mind if I called you Father?"

Julia reached up and squeezed Peter's hand as it lay on her shoulder.

"I would be delighted. I've wanted to be your father since the day you were born. I tried as best I could."

Bella went to him and took his free hand.

"You were always kind to me and I appreciated it very much. I never knew what I'd done to Ernst that he would ignore me so and then sell me. Now I know it's because he hated me. I reminded him of the love he could never have…my mother's love."

"We saw each other when we could, but it's been difficult," said Peter.

"You will never have to part again, now that Ernst had the good sense to kill himself. The bastard. I've have killed him if I could for selling me to that horrible, vicious troll of a man. Saying Rockwell was a man is saying an untruth, but I don't have the words for what he was," said Bella. Just the thought of the man made her stomach turn.

"We all know what you mean, my love," said Alex. "Now, shall we take that stroll?" He pointed behind them, at the garden.

Bella walked to Alex and took the hand he extended to her. "Yes. I'd like that very much."

CHAPTER 16

Bella held on to Alex's arm and leaned into him as they walked.

"I missed you," Alex said softly. "I was afraid I wouldn't get to you before you were terrorized completely."

"And I was afraid you were dead, though I prayed I was wrong. I didn't know if there was anyone who would come after me. I tried to get the seamstress to send word to Mother, but he made sure she couldn't do anything but sew on the dress. She was a captive in her own shop until that hideous gown was done."

"Are you all right, Bella? I feared he might hurt you, knowing how stubborn you can be." He smiled. "And I'm glad you're so stubborn, but are you and the baby all right?"

She stopped and looked up at her husband, knowing he was feeling vulnerable because he hadn't kept Rockwell's goons from kidnapping her.

"I'm fine. The baby is fine. We're back here with you. I love you, Alex, with my whole being. You and the children are my life."

"And you and the children are mine. I don't know what I'd do…"

She put two fingers gently over his lips.

"Shh. We will never have to know. We are together now, forever."

Bella lifted herself up and kissed her handsome husband. His daily growth of whiskers, rough on her tender cheek.

"I'm ready, Alex. Make love to me. Take away the memory of what he nearly did to me."

"Come with me."

He took her hand and started for the house.

"No, make love to me now. Right here, on the grass. It's warm out and no one in the house can see us. Look, you can't see the library from here. We're safe."

She reached up and caressed his face, her hand cupped his jaw.

"Love me, Alex."

"Whatever you want, my love. Whenever you want. Wherever you want."

He took off his jacket and laid it on the ground. Then he started unbuttoning her dress. She wore only a chemise with it and he untied the laces, revealing her body.

"I've missed these lovelies, too. I think they are larger since you are with child."

"They are more sensitive than ever."

He bent and kissed her mouth and then traveled on down her neck until he reached her breast. He took her nipple and ran the tip of his tongue over the hard little pebble.

She felt her body go liquid, and all her feelings concentrated on his mouth and her nipple, and then ignited her core into fiery flames.

"Now, Alex, don't make me wait."

"I want to love you slow and show you how much I love you."

"Slow later. Now I need you to fill me, to take away the memory of him over me. I need you to love me, now, Alex. Now."

He kissed her hard.

"Whatever you want, I shall do."

Alex left her for a moment and opened his pants, then he was back with her. Over her and in her.

All other thoughts left her mind at the feel of him making love to her.

Bella closed her eyes and felt only Alex and her mind was at peace.

Later they returned to the house and to their room where her husband made slow love to her all night long.

*****

Peter took about a week to make the necessary arrangements to be gone for an extended length of time.

"It's about time my managers earned the exorbitant salary I pay them," he said at breakfast on the morning they were to leave.

"It's worked out wonderfully, my love," said Julia. "Bella and I have taken the time to buy her clothes to get her through her entire pregnancy. And now she can take the linens and china that my grandmother handed down to her."

"Perhaps we should try and rent a stagecoach of our own from Cheyenne to Hope's Crossing," said Peter.

"I don't think you'll find any to rent," said Sam. "But there'll be some nice carriages to buy for sure. Then when you go back to New York you can resell it back to the same company for less money than you paid, of course, but it would almost be like renting."

"Or you can just let me buy it," said Alex. "With the new baby and two girls already, I need something bigger than the buggy or the buckboard. A nice carriage would be perfect."

"We'll talk about who is buying what," said Peter with a grin. "And by the time we get to Cheyenne, you'll agree I should give it to you as a wedding present."

Sam barked a laugh.

"He's got you there, Alex."

"All right," said Alex. "You two can give us the carriage as a wedding...and birthing present for the baby."

"Oh no, you don't. I have something completely different in mind for the baby and have already bought it," said Julia.

"At this rate we might need two carriages. One just for luggage," groaned Alex.

"Don't worry, my love. I didn't let her get too carried away. Besides," said Bella with a grin. "She's shipping whatever we can't take with us.

*****

August 28, 1874
Hope's Crossing, Montana Territory

Alex ran his hand up and down Bella's bare back.

She loved this time of the morning. They'd just made love and now she was pretending to go back to sleep.

"Are you sure your parents are ready to get married tomorrow?"

Bella turned over so Alex's hand now caressed her rounded stomach and breasts.

"They are fine, anxious even. What about you? Are you ready for the double ceremony?"

"We are already married," he groused with a scowl. "I only agreed to this church wedding because you wanted to walk down the aisle with your mother."

"I know you did, and yes, we are already married, or I'd never be in this condition." She patted the bulge of her stomach where the baby grew. "I always dreamed of a church wedding, though. And I bought the most beautiful dress while I was in New York. I don't want to wait for another four months, or longer, to wear it. I can barely get into it now."

"Are you sure you still can? You've expanded somewhat since we left New York."

Bella sat up, the sheet lying at her waist.

"I didn't even think of that. Oh Alex, what will I wear then?"

"One of the other beautiful dresses you bought. They are all lovely. What about that dark green one?"

"Which one? I have more than one. I couldn't stop Mother from buying me every dress I liked. I got to the point I quit having an opinion of the dresses at all."

"I know." He smiled at her. "I mean whichever green one fits you now."

She got up and walked to the closet which was full to overflowing with her dresses. Her favorite was a blue one, with off the shoulder sleeves and a fitted waist. But it wouldn't fit her now, which if she'd been thinking she would have known.

She'd discovered she couldn't look at purple or pink dresses since her ordeal with Rockwell. And blue, which had been her least favorite color before, was now her favorite color.

Alex's suit hung over the back of one of the chairs in the room.

Bella had brought a trunk full of dresses that now resided in Alex's closet. She pulled out three dark green dresses from within it. One was velvet and was intended to be her Christmas dress. She couldn't wear that one for a long time. The second was a simple cotton gown which was cut so she could wear it though the rest of her pregnancy. The last one was silk and a rich emerald green.

"That's the one," said Alex. "Can you wear that one?"

"I don't know."

She slipped the dress over her head and pulled it down. The empire waist was such she could wear it now and it looked like for some time in the future.

"Come button me up, please."

Alex did as he was bade and got out of bed, stark naked. She had a hard time keeping her eyes looking straight ahead when she knew her husband was ready to make love again.

"There," he patted her bottom. "All done. Turn around and let me see."

She saw his face light up as he smiled.

"That's the winner. See for yourself."

He pointed at the mirror over the bureau.

She turned and looked at herself. The dress was beautiful and her skin looked porcelain against the vivid color.

She gazed at Alex in the mirror as he stood behind her, his hands wrapped around her waist. Or at least, where her waist used to be.

"It's supposed to be bad luck for the groom to see the bride before the wedding."

"Too late." He nuzzled her neck. "We are already married, and I've seen all of you, naked. What kind of luck is that? Damned good luck, if you ask me."

She laughed and bent her neck, allowing him better access for his kisses.

He chuckled. "Like that, do you?"

"You know I do."

"How about we get you back out of this dress and you let me do wonderful things to your body? It's early yet."

She nodded, loving the feeling of his lips on her skin too much to give voice to her assent.

Alex led her back to the bed, slowly unbuttoned her dress, kissing every new inch of skin that was revealed.

"You are insatiable."

"Only where you are concerned. I will never get enough of you. Not for all the one hundred years, or more, of our marriage."

"One hundred years! Goodness. I'll be an old woman. You're won't want me when I'm one hundred and twenty-three."

"You'll still be a spring chicken compared to me at one hundred and thirty-one. I don't care how old or gray or wrinkled we get. I'll always want and love you."

"I love you too, and as much as I would love to get back in bed with you," she gathered her hair over one shoulder baring her neck for him. "We have little ones in the adjoining room that are probably awake and needing for us to get them dressed and fed before this wedding at ten o'clock."

"I look forward to the day when they can do all that for themselves."

"You'll be waiting a long time." She rubbed circles on her tummy. "I doubt very seriously this will be the last baby we have."

He walked back to the bed and fell back upon it.

"But I do so like the part where we make those babies."

She turned to face him.

"As do I, my love, as do I."

A knock sounded on the door.

"Mama. Daddy." Violet's wee voice came from the other side. "Can we come in?"

Alex covered himself with the blankets.

"Yes, girls, you can come in now," said Bella who still wore the emerald dress.

"We knocked like you told us to," said Vi, her hand rubbing the sleep out of her eyes.

Both girls were in long flannel nightgowns and socks, though the beautiful paisley patterned blue carpet kept the floor from being cold. They'd gotten this hotel room specifically so the girls wouldn't have to be in the same room with them. At one time, Effie and Lavernia had lived together in this suite, but with the sisters now feuding, Effie decided she didn't want to be in this big room anymore and rented it to families.

"Yeah. Vi made me wait. I wanted to come in but she said, "Mama made us promise to knock first.'"

"And Vi was right. I'm so happy you remembered."

"You look awful pretty, Mama," said Rose. "Is that cause yer gettin' married to Daddy?"

"Yes, and your grandma and grandpa are getting married, too."

"And Rose and me are in the weddin', ain't we?" asked Vi.

"It's aren't we and yes, you are. You are our ring girls. Rose will have Daddy's ring for Mama, and Vi will have Grandpa's ring for Grandma."

"I gots the biggest ring," said Vi.

"No, sir. Mama's ring is the biggest," said Rose.

"Hush, both of you. The rings are perfect for Grandma and Mama. I love my ring from your Daddy, and Grandma feels the same about her ring from Grandpa. We both have exactly what we want."

Alex sat up. "Are you sure, love? I can get you a fancy ring if you want one."

"No. I want to be able to wear my ring all the time, including when I'm doing my chores. Can you see me trying to wear my mother's ring and gather eggs? It would get caught on the nests and get full of who knows what." She shook her head. "No, thank you. Not for me."

He grinned up at her. "That's my practical bride. Always thinking ahead."

"Yes, I am. I'm glad you recognize how lucky you are."

"Weren't we just talking about how lucky I am?"

He cocked his eyebrow and gave her the wickedest grin.

If the girls hadn't been there, she'd have been sorely tempted to take advantage of her handsome husband.

"I'm taking the girls to their room to dress. While we're gone, I expect you to get dressed as well."

"Yes, ma'am." He saluted her.

Bella ushered the girls into their room and helped them dress. Then she did their hair in ponytails tied with ribbon to match their dresses. Pink for Rose and lavender blue for Violet. They looked so sweet in their little dresses with three layers of ruffles in the skirt and lace at the collar and the cuffs.

Her beautiful daughters. Growing up so fast. They would be five before the new baby arrived. A little older and a little more mature, so maybe they would get along with their new brother or sister. They did love

Jo's son, but he wasn't brand new and needed Mama all the time.

Alex came to the connecting door.

"Can you help me with this cravat? I hate tying these things."

"Of course, come here," said Bella.

She tied his tie for him with a few quick motions then ran her hand down the front and smoothed any wrinkles.

"You look very handsome, husband."

He bent to kiss her.

"Thank you, wife."

*****

The church was packed with all their friends and neighbors.

Peter and Alex waited in the front of the church, one on either side of Reverend Parker.

Violet and Rose were the first ones up the aisle. They walked very solemnly to the front and handed their rings to the men. Violet to her grandfather and Rose to her father, then both girls went and sat with Sam and Jo.

Next were Bella and Julia. They walked arm-in-arm. Bella in her beautiful emerald green silk dress and Julia resplendent in a deep purple dress with open skirt gathered over the bustle and a lavender underskirt. The bodice was cut low enough to show some décolletage and provide a perfect frame for the diamond necklace Peter had given her as a wedding gift.

When Reverend Parker asked "who gives these women away?" Bella and Julia said together, "I do." They then parted and went to stand next to their husbands-to-be.

"Dearly beloved," intoned the reverend.

Before she knew it, Bella was answering "I do." She was married again to Alex. Her one true love. The man who came after her when she was stolen from him. The man who shared his daughters with her. The man who answered every one of her prayers without even knowing what they were.

EPILOGUE

August 28, 1875

"Mama!" Vi ran into the kitchen from outside. "They're here. Gramma and Grandpa are here."

Bella wiped her hands on her apron and checked the crib in the corner. Peter James Hastings was still sleeping, with Maddie the cat curled at his feet. At Vi's shouting, Maddie had lifted his head and looked around. Seeing nothing that would hurt his baby he lay back down.

PJ, as they called him, was almost nine months old and when he was awake was constantly on the move, crawling everywhere and getting into everything.

"You go on and greet your Mama," said Poppy. "Me and Maddie got little PJ covered."

"Thank you, Poppy."

Bella walked to the front door and out on to the porch. Jack B drove the carriage and Alex was inside with her parents. They had returned for their anniversary.

The coach pulled up in front, the door opened and Alex jumped down. He reached back and she saw her mother descend from the coach.

Bella ran down the steps to her mother, who when she turned, Bella could see was very pregnant.

"Mama?"

"Bella, my darling," Julia said walking forward. "Peter wanted to stay in town in case the baby decides to come, but I insisted that if I could travel seven days in a stagecoach and not have this baby, riding in the carriage to the ranch will not hurt either—"

Julia stopped abruptly.

"I could be wrong about that. Alex, I think you better send someone for the doctor, my water just broke."

"Don't take another step." Peter scooped

Julia up and carried her into the house.

Bella raced them to the door. "Follow me, Peter. Your room is ready. Alex, have Poppy boil some water and bring towels to the guest room."

She lifted her skirts, ran up the stairs just in front of Peter, and took him to the first room on the right side of the hall.

Bella turned down the covers. "Peter, let her stand so I can get her dress off. Mama, you'll be in your chemise and that's all."

"I remember from your birth. Just help me to bed."

They left Julia's clothes in a pile on the floor and she leaned on Bella for the short walk to the bed.

"How in the world did this happen at your age?" asked Bella.

"I'm only forty, Bella. You forget I was just sixteen when you were born. Peter and I didn't dare hope we could have another child and—"

A labor pain, followed by deep breathing cut Julia's explanation short.

When the pain had passed, Bella checked the clock on the bureau and noted the time.

"As I was saying, then when I

discovered I was expecting we were overjoyed. I have to admit, I wondered how you would take it having a sister or brother younger than your children and I decided you would be fine with it. Was I correct?"

"Of course, I will love having a sister or brother. What are you naming the baby?"

"Sophia if it's a girl, after Peter's aunt, and Howard if it's a boy, after Peter's father. They are good strong names I think."

"They are fine names. I'm getting used to the idea that I have a whole family now, with aunts and uncles and cousins."

She waved her hand. "Speaking of which, this time next year, your family has to come to New York. We are planning a family get together that will include all of Peter's relatives."

"I don't know. This is the time of year Alex is usually pretty busy, bringing the herd down from the high pastures."

Julia frowned. "He's here now."

"That's because we knew you were coming, and he has the men bringing in the cows."

"So, it's logical for me to assume he can have the same thing happen next year, and the men will bring in the herd. Oww."

Julia stopped again as a contraction hit.

Bella again checked the time. Fifteen minutes had passed. She should have plenty of time for the doctor to arrive, especially with Jack B riding to get him.

Alex kept Peter in the parlor, playing poker for beans.

"This is your first time isn't it?"

"Yes, Julia had been married off to Ernst. She never tried to hide the fact that Ernst was not the father. She hated being married to the man, but for Bella's sake, they pretended. I pretended. Every time I saw Bella, it was all I could do not to take her in my arms and hug her."

"Looks like things finally worked out for you. Bella said she's never seen her mother as happy as she was on your wedding day."

"I was the same way. We were finally getting what we'd wanted for more than twenty-four years." Peter stopped, set his cards on the table and looked at the ceiling. "Does it always take so long?"

"This isn't long yet. We still have a ways to go."

Three hours later, they were still playing cards when Jack B rode into the yard. He came into the house.

"The doc is right behind me. Should be here in a few minutes."

"That's wonderful news," said Alex. "Bella is ready for the doctor to be here, I think. She wasn't looking forward to having to deliver this baby."

"And she won't have to now that I'm here," said Doctor Kilarney. "Where is my patient?"

"Upstairs, first door on the right."

The doctor headed right up. "Tell Poppy to bring hot water as soon as possible. I like to clean up before I deliver."

About an hour and a half later, Bella came flying down the stairs.

"She's here. Father, you have a little girl and I have a sister. Mama is asking for you."

"Excuse me." Peter heaved a big sigh of relief, stood and ran toward the stairs.

Bella put her arms around Alex's neck.

"Can you believe it? I have a baby sister. If my mother is any indication, we could be having children for a long time to come."

He held her by the waist.

"We'll take as many children as the good Lord gives us. I love you, Bella Hastings."

She rose on tiptoe, and he lowered his head to meet her questing lips.

"I love you, Alex Hastings. For forever and a day."

*****

September 4, 1875

Bella and Alex hosted a Saturday picnic and horse race at their home. Most of the town came for the roasted pig and beef and to see Bella and Alex finally race.

Jesse brought the buggy with the matched grays.

Bella walked out of the house wearing her dark red riding outfit and her riding boots. The split skirt allowed her to ride astride.

They both saddled their respective horses, and Bella thought her husband was a little surprised at her knowledge.

"This will be different for me as I'm not used to these kinds of saddles, but I still believe I can beat you." *Lord, I hope so. I really want to ride that black stallion.*

"We'll see. Same stakes we discussed?"

"Yes. When I win, I get to ride the black."

"And when I win, you stop pestering me

to ride the black."

"It's a bet." She held out her hand.

Alex took her hand and shook it, then pulled her in for a quick kiss.

"Alex. We have company." She looked around at all their family and friends who were watching with interest.

"Each of whom understand that if I win you may not want to kiss me for awhile."

They mounted.

Sam fired a shot into the air.

The horses took off, their riders leaning flat over their mounts' necks.

They ran for about a half mile, to a post, rounding the post and riding back toward Sam at the finish line.

Bella rode hard. Her blood raced through her veins and she remembered Champion and running him in the park. Her gray was steady and winded when they finished a full five seconds before Alex. The crowd watching erupted in cheers and applause.

"I win. You have to let me ride the black."

She saw Alex's face, recognized real fear upon it and softened her declaration.

"But only when you can ride with me."

He visibly relaxed.

"Deal?"

"Deal."

She handed the reins to her horse to Jack B.

Alex did the same.

Bella walked to Alex.

"I don't want you to fear for me. The idea of this race was to show you I am an accomplished horseman. Nothing else. If you really don't want me to ride the black, I won't. I don't want to cause you any anguish."

Alex pulled her into his arms.

"Thank you for understanding. We'll talk more about riding the black stallion. I do believe you can handle him, but I can't stop the fear that what happened to Kate could happen to you."

"Then I won't ride him. When we ride together, I'll ride Stargazer and you can ride the black. I just want a horse with some spirit. I don't need a gentle mare with a soft mouth."

"Agreed."

He kissed her. *Hard.*

And she met him with the same ferocity, happy with the concession of her riding his beautiful bay stallion, Stargazer.

"I love you, Alex and now that the race is over, there is something I should tell you."

"What is that?"

"We're having another baby."

"I wondered when you'd tell me."

"How'd you know?"

"You're breasts are bigger and more sensitive."

She leaned back, his arms encircling her. "How do you feel about having another child?"

"I will love any child we have, you know that."

"I'm glad." *I was worried you might not want more children.* "I was almost afraid to tell you."

"You don't ever have to be afraid to tell me anything.".

"I won't from now on. I'm a little scared about it myself."

"Why? You're a wonderful mother."

"But we'll have two in diapers. You have any idea how much laundry will be and…"

"Shh." He placed two fingers lightly on her lips. "I remember with Rose and Violet. If we need to, we'll hire someone just to do laundry. Don't worry."

She sighed.

"I love you, Alex Hastings."

"And I you. For forever and a day."

ABOUT THE AUTHOR

Cynthia Woolf is the award winning and best-selling author of twenty-one historical western romance books and two short stories with more books on the way. She was born in Denver, Colorado and raised in the mountains west of Golden. She spent her early years running wild around the mountain side with her friends.

Their closest neighbor was about one quarter of a mile away, so her little brother was her playmate and her best friend. That fierce friendship lasted until his death in 2006.

Cynthia loves writing and reading romance. Her first western romance Tame A Wild Heart, was inspired by the story her mother told her of meeting Cynthia's father on a ranch in Creede, Colorado. Although Tame A Wild Heart takes place in Creede that is the only similarity between the stories. Her father was a cowboy not a bounty hunter and her mother was a nursemaid (called a nanny now) not the ranch owner.

Cynthia credits her wonderfully supportive husband Jim and the great friends she's made at CRW for saving her sanity and allowing her to explore her creativity.

TITLES AVAILABLE

THORPE'S MAIL-ORDER BRIDE, Montana Sky

Series (Kindle Worlds)
GENEVIEVE: Bride of Nevada, American Mail-Order
Brides Series
THE HUNTER BRIDE – Hope's Crossing, Book 1
THE REPLACEMENT BRIDE – Hope's Crossing,
Book 2
THE STOLEN BRIDE – Hope's Crossing, Book 3
GIDEON – The Surprise Brides
MAIL ORDER OUTLAW – The Brides of Tombstone,
Book 1
MAIL ORDER DOCTOR – The Brides of Tombstone,
Book 2
MAIL ORDER BARON – The Brides of Tombstone,
Book 3
NELLIE – The Brides of San Francisco 1
ANNIE – The Brides of San Francisco 2
CORA – The Brides of San Francisco 3
JAKE (Book 1, Destiny in Deadwood series)
LIAM (Book 2, Destiny in Deadwood series)
ZACH (Book 3, Destiny in Deadwood series)
CAPITAL BRIDE (Book 1, Matchmaker & Co. series)
HEIRESS BRIDE (Book 2, Matchmaker & Co. series)
FIERY BRIDE (Book 3, Matchmaker & Co. series)
TAME A WILD HEART (Book 1, Tame series)
TAME A WILD WIND (Book 2, Tame series)
TAME A WILD BRIDE (Book 3, Tame series)
TAME A HONEYMOON HEART (novella, Tame
series)

WEBSITE – http://cynthiawoolf.com/

NEWSLETTER - http://bit.ly/1qBWhFQ

DISCARD

42342728R00160

Made in the USA
Lexington, KY
15 June 2019